Welcome to the Secret World of Alex Mack!

Well, it seemed like a good idea at the time! A weekend camping trip with my friends (and Scott!) that would help me earn extra credit for my science grade. Except my parents and Annie were recruited as chaperones. Robyn thinks she's seen a bear! And he's not the only one lurking out in the woods—Vince and Dave are sniffing around too. Forget the great outdoors—get me back to civilization! Let me explain. . . .

I'm Alex Mack. I was just another average kid until my first day of junior high.

One minute I'm walking home from school—the next there's a *crash!* A truck from the Paradise Valley Chemical plant overturns in front of me, and I'm drenched in some weird chemical.

And since then—well, nothing's been the same. I can move objects with my mind, shoot electrical charges through my fingertips, and morph into a liquid shape . . . which is handy when I get in a tight spot!

My best friend, Ray, thinks it's cool. And my sister Annie thinks I'm a science project.

They're the only two people who know about my new powers. I can't let anyone else find out—not even my parents—because I know the chemical plant wants to find me and turn me into some experiment.

But you know something? I guess I'm not so average anymore!

The Secret World of Alex Mack™

Alex, You're Glowing!
Bet You Can't!
Bad News Babysitting!
Witch Hunt!
Mistaken Identity!
Cleanup Catastrophe!
Take a Hike!
Go for the Gold!
Poison in Paradise!
Zappy Holidays! (Super Edition)
Junkyard Jitters!
Frozen Stiff!
I Spy!
High Flyer!
Milady Alex!

Available from MINSTREL Books

Take a Hike!

Cathy East Dubowski

A
MINSTREL®
BOOK

Published by POCKET BOOKS
New York   London   Toronto   Sydney   Tokyo   Singapore

This book is a work of fiction. Names, characters, places and incidents are products of the author's imagination or are used fictitiously. Any resemblance to actual events or locales or persons, living or dead, is entirely coincidental.

A MINSTREL PAPERBACK *Original*

A Minstrel Book published by
POCKET BOOKS, a division of Simon & Schuster Inc.
1230 Avenue of the Americas, New York, NY 10020

ISBN: 0-671-56309-2

First Minstrel Books printing June 1996

10 9 8 7 6 5 4 3

Cover photography by Blake Little

Printed in the U.S.A.

To Mark—
who keeps me down to earth,
helps me hike the trails,
and always reminds me to look at the stars

Take a Hike!

CHAPTER 1

Alex Mack squirmed against the thick, rusty chains that bound her to her desk in Mr. Hendricks's science class.

Tick-tick! Tick-tick! Tick-tick!

BONG! BONG!

Alex glanced up at the clock.

Two a.m.!?

Alex stared out the window. Moonlight reflected off the schoolyard's deserted bike rack.

She'd been here for hours! She'd missed supper, her favorite TV show. And it was way past her bedtime. Her parents must be frantic!

Would this science test never end?

"Alex! Hurry up! I'm waiting for you!"

Alex rubbed her sleepy eyes and squinted toward the doorway. Standing in the darkened hall, Scott Greene waved at her through thick iron prison bars that blocked the door.

Now she remembered: He'd asked her to go with him to the Half-Life, the coolest after-school hangout in Paradise Valley—even though he was a ninth-grader and she was only in the eighth grade. He was going to treat her to some curly fries. And he had something important to ask her. . . .

But she couldn't go until she finished this test!

Alex tried to scribble down an answer—*any* answer—but she couldn't lift her arm an inch. Her hand weighed a ton!

She sneaked a look at the clock again. Now a skull and cross bones leered at her, its bony arms pointing out the time . . .

Four a.m.!

"ALEXANDRA MACK!" a deep voice rumbled. Mr. Hendricks! "Time is running *out-out-out*. . . ."

Alex sneaked a look at her teacher. His thick

spectacles glowed like headlights. And why was he wearing a *police officer's* uniform—at school?

Alex stared at her test paper.

The words scrambled across the page like bugs in a Raid attack. She tried to scoop them back onto the paper.

Her number 2 pencil squirmed in her leaden hand. But it wasn't a pencil. It was . . .

A snake with fangs!

Alex flung it across the room.

The chains tightened around her, choking her . . .

"Scott!" she cried frantically. "Help me!"

"I can't, Alex! I can't get in!"

There was only one way out. Alex would have to use her secret powers. The only problem: which one?

She could zap the lock on the prison door. Or she could close her eyes, morph into a silvery thick liquid, and ooze out of her chains.

But wait! Maybe Scott wouldn't want to take an oozy, gurgling puddle of silvery Jell-O to the Half-Life. Maybe a gooey Alex would gross him out.

A little fingertip fireworks, on the other hand, might actually impress him.

Better zap! Alex quickly decided. Blast the door open. Then Scott could help her escape.

Alex started to wiggle her fingertips—

"Don't you dare!"

Alex froze. Her head whipped around. Stepping out from behind Mr. Hendricks, her older sister, Annie, glared at her. And she was wearing a police officer's uniform, too!

"Remember, Alex," Annie warned, wagging her finger in Alex's face. "You can't use your powers in public! You can't let anyone know . . . *can't let anyone know . . .*"

But Alex no longer cared. All she could think about was getting out of this awful class.

Twisting in her chains, she wiggled the tips of her stiff fingers.

Zap! Lightning-like flashes blasted the iron bars. Sparks showered the room.

"Al-e-e-e-e-x!" Scott shouted.

Alex ducked her head as the room filled with smoke.

Someone grabbed her shoulders.

"Alex!"

Now someone was shaking her.

"Alex! Snap out of it!"

4

Alex slowly opened one eye.

Her face was smooshed into the crook of her arm. A tiny dribble of drool trickled from the corner of her mouth.

"Alex!" Annie gave her another shake. "Alex, get up. You're going to be late!"

Alex sat up slowly and shoved her long dirty-blond hair out of her face. "Where's . . . Mr. Hendricks?" she mumbled.

Annie rolled her dark brown eyes. "At school, I expect. Which is where you should be headed."

Alex opened her other eye.

She wasn't at Danielle Atron Junior High School. She wasn't in Mr. Hendricks's science class.

She was at home, in the kitchen.

She stared at the table in front of her.

No science test.

Just a bowl of soggy breakfast cereal that had lost all its snap, crackle, and pop.

Schoolwork! She knew it was getting her down. But now she was even having nightmares about it—at the breakfast table!

Alex let out a big groan, poked her spoon into her cereal, and took a mushy bite. If Mr. Hendricks and the science test had been a dream, then so had her date with Scott at the Half-Life. *I should have known it couldn't be true....*

"By the way, Alex," Annie said dryly. "You just zapped the toaster. Care for some burnt toast?"

Alex studied the appliance. It had a slight scorch mark on its shiny side. She must have zapped it while she daydreamed "Oops! Sorry."

"I think the toaster is all right," Annie said. "But what if Mom or Dad had seen you?"

Alex yawned. "Where are they, anyway?"

"They're running late." Annie frowned as she tapped a stack of papers on the tabletop to neaten them, then slipped them into a gray report cover. "It's not like them."

Alex glared at her sister. Her shoulder-length dark brown hair was freshly shampooed and brushed till it shone. Her clothes were neat and attractive—though a little on the boring side, Alex thought.

Annie looked bright-eyed and beautiful and ready to tackle the world.

As usual.

Annie was definitely a morning person. *Just another way we're completely different*, Alex thought grumpily.

She and sixteen-year-old Annie shared the same parents and the same room—but very little else. Annie had inherited their father's scientific genius and their mother's energy. Teachers adored her. Awards lined her side of their room.

Alex, on the other hand, thought early birds *deserved* to catch worms, and she figured noon would be a reasonable time for homeroom to begin. Teachers didn't exactly hate her. But when they saw her grades, they often couldn't help but exclaim, "Alex, why can't you be more like your sister, Annie?"

Annie took her breakfast dishes to the sink to rinse them. Suddenly she turned around and stared at her sleepy sister with a worried frown. "Hey, Alex," she said gently. "Are you feeling okay?"

"I'm fine."

Alex and Annie did not have a lot in common. And they didn't always get along—like a lot of sisters, Alex supposed. But she knew her sister was really concerned about her. Especially since the accident.

On the first day of junior high school, she'd almost been creamed by a truck from the Paradise Valley Chemical plant. When the truck swerved and hit a fire hydrant, Alex had been accidentally drenched by an experimental chemical called GC 161.

The driver had tried to catch her, but she'd escaped—only to discover that the icky golden goo was not only gross but had caused her to develop some outrageous powers. She could zap things, float things, and morph into a sort of silvery Jell-O puddle that could sneak through pipes and under doorways.

I guess I'm not so ordinary anymore! Alex had thought at the time. *These powers are going to change my life!*

And they had. Just not exactly the way Alex had expected.

Annie decided they shouldn't tell anyone. Not even their parents. Only Alex's best friend, Raymond Alvarado, knew her secret, because, of course, he wouldn't tell. Annie wouldn't let her confide in her other best friends, Robyn

Russo and Nicole Wilson. That was the hardest part.

Even worse, they'd learned that Danielle Atron, the chief executive officer of Paradise Valley Chemical, wanted her—bad. She had ordered two plant employees to work full-time to find the GC 161 kid. Vince, her coldhearted head of security. And likable—but not very bright— Dave, who'd been driving the truck when the accident happened.

Annie feared that if they ever caught Alex, they'd turn her into a human guinea pig and perform all sorts of horrible experiments on her. Alex's life would be ruined.

So now plain old Alex was very special. Only nobody could know anything about it.

Now she had fabulous powers like a superhero in a science fiction novel. Only she still had to do homework, take out the garbage, and worry about being popular. She still got zits.

Annie the scientific genius had performed all kinds of experiments on her. She'd told Alex that, except for her strange new powers, she was okay. Probably.

At least . . . she was *pretty* sure.

Still, Alex knew Annie worried about her.

Annie rushed over and felt Alex's forehead. "Any symptoms? Weakness, fever, tiredness? Maybe I should run some more tests. . . ."

"Annie, I'm fine, really!" Alex said. "Well, not exactly. I do have a problem. But it's got nothing to do with the GC 161."

Annie sat down. "What, then?"

"It's school!"

"Alex, you *always* have a problem with school."

"But lately it's been worse," Alex insisted. "The school year's almost over. But instead of easing up a little, the teachers are really piling on the homework. It's like they're having a contest to see who can give us the most work before we escape for the summer. And I think Mr. Hendricks is going to win."

"Yeah, I remember his class," Annie said with a fond smile. "He always did give a lot of homework. It was invigorating."

Give me a break! Alex thought. "Well, I feel like I'm in jail. I'm even having nightmares about it."

"Alex, your only *real* problem is your attitude," Annie lectured. "You need to stop regarding your schoolwork as your enemy. Think of it as a challenge. A mountain to climb!''

"Yeah, right," Alex mumbled. "What would *you* know about a challenge, Annie? School's easy for you."

"That's not true, Alex," Annie insisted. "But I like school. And I work hard. Very hard. Unlike you, I put in the hours. That's what makes it *seem* easy."

"Uh-huh," Alex responded, not convinced.

"Besides, there are only a few more weeks to go."

"But I feel like I've been in eighth grade for years!" Alex yawned and buried her face in her balled-up sweatshirt. One of her teachers had once said that Thomas Edison, inventor of the lightbulb, was a rotten student. But when he grew up and became a genius, he got his work done by taking quick little catnaps.

Just how long is a catnap, anyway? Alex wondered. Maybe she could squeeze one in before she *really* had to leave.

Just then Barbara Mack rushed into the kitchen, reading a file of papers and brushing her shoulder-length blond hair. She dropped her brush into her purse to pour herself a mug of coffee, then sat down at the table—still reading.

" 'Morning, girls," she said with a yawn. She hurriedly shuffled through her papers and jabbed some numbers into a pocket calculator.

Seconds later George Mack dashed in, grabbed a mug of coffee, and sat down beside his wife. " 'Morning, everybody," he mumbled through a yawn. He set his laptop computer on the table and flipped up the top.

Barbara Mack was a busy public relations executive. George Mack was a top research scientist at Paradise Valley Chemical.

Both loved their work. But they'd been working even longer hours than usual lately. Alex's mom was big on salads and whole grains and stuff—but they'd had frozen pizzas for supper twice this week.

Barbara Mack grabbed for her coffee mug.

George Mack grabbed for his.

But they grabbed the same mug—and tugged.

Coffee splashed across the kitchen table.

Annie grabbed some paper towels as Mrs. Mack scooped up her papers and Mr. Mack scooted his computer out of the way.

Only then did Mr. and Mrs. Mack really look at each other—and sigh.

Mrs. Mack pulled off her reading glasses. "Boy, George, do we need a break!"

"You're absolutely right, Barbara," Mr. Mack agreed. He closed his laptop and sighed. "I've just been working too hard on this GC 161 project. It has such exciting possibilities. And Danielle has really been pushing for some results. If only . . ."

Annie's ears perked up at the mention of GC 161. "If only what, Dad?"

George Mack shook his head. "If only I could figure out what GC 161 can be used for. It could have the capacity to alter human genetic structure!"

Annie shot Alex a nervous glance. Unfortunately, Alex had dozed off again.

They'd come close to telling their parents a few times that their daughter Alex had been doused with a dose of GC 161 herself. But George Mack's boss was Danielle Atron. And Barbara Mack often worked with her on publicity for the plant. The girls didn't want to do anything that might cause the government to close down the plant. Then both their parents would be out of a job. And so would most of Paradise Valley!

Besides, they were afraid that the plant would find out about Alex. The fewer people who knew about her, the better.

"Don't worry, Dad," Annie said brightly, patting her father on the arm. "You'll figure it out eventually."

"I hope so," he said, shaking his head.

Alex propped her head up on one hand and mumbled sleepily, "What did you say, Dad?"

George Mack grinned affectionately at his second daughter. "I said it's time for school, Alex."

Alex mumbled goodbye as she grabbed her pack and headed for the door.

"It might be smart to open your eyes on the way there!" Annie called out.

Crash! The sound of smashing trashcans made George and Barbara Mack wince.

Alex poked her sleepy head back inside the door. "Uh, I'm okay!" Then she spotted a paper bag on the counter. "Oops! Forgot my lunch."

Her parents exchanged a concerned glance.

"Alex, honey, are you okay?" Barbara Mack asked. "Is something wrong?"

"Nothing that summer vacation won't cure," Annie teased as she picked up her own books.

Alex made a playful face at her sister as she headed once more for the back door.

"We're entirely too busy as a family these days," Barbara Mack announced to her family. "We don't even know what's going on with you girls at school—especially you, Alex."

"I agree," George Mack said. "We need to spend more time together as a family."

"Sure, Dad. Maybe this summer. 'Bye!" The kitchen door slammed as Alex raced off.

No need to worry, Alex told herself. *They'll forget about this family time stuff by suppertime.*

CHAPTER 2

Outside, Alex squinted in the early-morning sun and made faces at the cheery chirping birds as she plodded down the sidewalk.

Slam! Her best friend, Ray, wandered out of his house next door and joined her. His dark brown eyes were droopy, and his T-shirt was on inside-out.

A couple of houses down, Louis Driscoll joined them. His curly reddish-brown hair looked wilder than usual. And his shoelaces were untied.

Both guys looked as if they were sleepwalking.

Louis held his arms out in front and joked, "Zombie Kids Stalk to School."

Ray laughed. "You, too, huh? I could hardly drag myself out of bed this morning. By next week, Dad's going to have to use dynamite to get me up."

"School is so boring," Alex complained. "We really need a break."

"You said it, Alex," Ray agreed. "Something to take us away from it all. An adventure of some kind . . ."

"An adventure?" Louis exclaimed, pretending to be horrified. "No, no, no, no, Ray. Forget that! I see"—he squinted off into the distance—"a tropical beach. Palm trees. A large hammock. Lots of snacks. Maybe a big-screen TV."

As they headed into the schoolyard, Alex began to daydream about her perfect getaway adventure.

Going to the movies with Scott—and using a force field to lock everybody else out of the theater till they'd seen their top ten favorite movies of all time. *Perfect* . . .

Or sharing a pizza in . . . *Paris*, with Scott, while she zapped fireworks over the Eiffel Tower . . .

"Perfect!" Ray exclaimed.

Alex's daydreams disappeared like popped soap bubbles. "Huh?"

Ray was pointing at a notice on the school's main bulletin board:

TAKE A HIKE!

The Danielle Atron Junior High School Science and Nature Club is sponsoring "Explorations"—a weekend camping trip— as our end-of-the-year project.

The trip is open to all eighth- and ninth-graders.

Challenge yourself!

Explore nature as well as your outdoor skills!

Alex read some of the planned activities out loud: "Plant and animal identification. Camping and hiking skills. First-aid workshops—"

"And tubing on the river!" Ray shouted. "All right!" He scribbled his name on the sign-up sheet. "I'm in."

Alex shot Ray a look of disbelief. "Are you crazy?"

18

"Come on, it'll be fun!" Ray said. "We'll get away from the books for a couple of days and hang out in the fresh air. It's probably our last chance to have some fun before we start studying for final exams."

Alex shook her head. "Camping is not exactly my thing, Ray."

Louis wrinkled his freckled nose, thinking. "I don't know, Ray. I was hoping for something a little more tropical. A little more laid-back."

"Hey," Ray said, pointing at the poster. " 'Challenge yourself.' I think it sounds cool."

"Well, count me out," Alex said. "I think all this 'adventure' stuff is just a lame cover-up for the truth."

"Say what?" Ray asked.

"Science!" Alex exclaimed. "Mr. Hendricks is the Science Club adviser—remember? So you know this trip is just going to be one long science class. And Ray, you know how much I hate science! I'd rather stay home and be bored."

"Anything's better than that!" Louis shuddered. "There's a rule at my house: 'Get *bored*, get *chored!*' Yeech! Besides, now that I think of it, we might have a better shot at talking our parents into *this* trip. To grown-ups, 'educational school trip' has a much better ring to it than 'Hawaiian cruise.' We could still take our hammocks.''

"Now you're talking!" Ray said, slapping him five. He passed his pen to Louis so he could sign up, too.

"Hey, guys!" Nicole called out cheerfully as she and Robyn joined them.

Robyn looked as if her Eveready batteries had finally worn down. She flipped her long red hair over her shoulder and pushed her rose-colored granny glasses up on her nose. "Is it the last day of school yet?"

Alex laughed. "Almost."

Nicole's eyes lit up when she spotted the notice on the bulletin board. "The Explorations trip! Oh, great! I've been waiting for this. Hey, are you guys signing up?"

"No way!" Robyn said quickly. "I'm allergic to camping." She began to count off on her fingers: "Let's see, there's mosquito bites, sunburn, sleeping on the cold hard ground, ticks, dirt, bear attacks—"

Alex giggled. "*Bear* attacks?"

Nicole jammed her fist on her hip and shook

her head. "Get real, Robyn. There are no bears in Paradise Valley."

"Oh yeah?" Robyn asked. "How can you be so sure? Have you looked under every rock, every tree?" She folded her arms and shook her head. "Life's dangerous enough as it is. I say, why go stomping around in the wilderness *looking* for ways to get hurt?"

"So life has risks." Nicole shrugged. "But if you don't jump into life with both feet, you're definitely gonna miss all the fun!"

Alex grinned. Her two best girlfriends were as different as peanut butter and jelly. But when you stuck them together, they made a fabulous combination. And they were just about as inseparable!

Nicole took the pen from Louis and wrote her name in big, bold caps. "A camping trip is a great way to get in touch with nature and recharge those brain cells. Come on, Alex. What do you say? It'll be a great way to rev up for final exams."

"Sorry, Nicole," Alex said with a grin. "I'm with Robyn this time. You couldn't *pay* me to go on this trip!"

"Hey, wait a minute!" Ray suddenly leaned over and peered at the bottom of the poster— and his eyes nearly popped out. "Listen to this! 'To receive extra credit toward your final science grade, see Mr. Hendricks.'"

Extra credit! That was something Alex could *definitely* use. She'd been struggling to make average grades in science all year. Which was especially humiliating, since her dad and her sister were finalists in the Albert Einstein act-alike contest. It was tempting, but . . .

"I repeat. I hate science," Alex said. "And I'm still not convinced a few points of extra credit are worth a weekend with Mr. Hendricks."

"Come on. He's not that bad."

Alex would know that voice anywhere. She spun around. Scott was standing right behind her, grinning.

"Are you guys signing up for the Explorations trip?"

"Uh, I don't know," Alex hedged. "I'm thinking about it."

"You really should go," Scott said. "We've planned tons of cool stuff to do. It'll be fun."

"That's right," Ray said. "You're club president."

Scott nodded. "The trip last year was awesome. So what do you say? Alex?"

Let's see, she thought. Extra credit in science. A weekend with all her friends—*away* from Annie and her parents and chores. And a chance to roast marshmallows with Scott beneath a sky full of stars?

Alex grinned. "You talked me into it!" She wrote her name down—right under Scott's.

"All right, Alex!" Ray cheered.

Now Alex and Nicole stared at Robyn.

Robyn groaned. "Okay, okay, I give up!" She wrote her name on the sign-up sheet. "I know I'm going to regret this. But, like, if I don't go, I can tell I'm going to be the only person left in town for the whole weekend!"

Alex and her friends laughed.

Just then Kelly Phillips strolled up and snaked her arm through Scott's. "Hi, everybody," the pretty ninth-grader said in a bright, friendly voice. "What's so funny?"

"Hi, Kelly," Scott said. "They're just signing up for the Science and Nature Club trip."

"You're coming, too? How nice," Kelly said with a small smile.

Alex winced.

Kelly was pretty popular, and she hung out with a cool crowd. But to Alex, she always sounded so fake. She usually had on this stunning (or was it *stunned-looking?*) smile—the one beauty contest finalists wore when they told judges they wanted to work for world peace and invent new uses for Tupperware.

Kelly had a problem with Alex, anyway. Alex would never forget the time she babysat for Kelly's monster of a little sister. The little brat had played with her father's wallet and lost it somewhere in the house. But Kelly made everybody at school think Alex had stolen it. She'd finally cleared her name. But she still got upset whenever she thought about it.

Kelly's fake smile was obvious to Alex and her friends. Scott never seemed to notice.

But then, that was one thing Alex really admired about Scott. He was probably the most popular guy at school. He was smart and cute and cool and had every right to be a total snob.

But he wasn't. He was nice to everybody.

Even Kelly.

Kelly was sort of Scott's girlfriend. But was it

Alex's imagination, or was Scott spending less time with her lately? Alex sighed. *Probably just wishful thinking.*

The bell rang. Kids scattered to their classes like bugs in a Raid attack—which reminded Alex of her dream.

Ugh. First period—science with Mr. Hendricks.

"Don't forget the club meeting after school tomorrow!" Scott said with a wink as he got swept down the hall.

"I'll be there!" Alex called after him. *Even though I'd rather be going to the movies or eating pizza in Paris.*

Alex couldn't wait to tell her parents—scratch that—*ask* her parents about going on the trip.

But when her parents rushed through the door that night, they seemed awfully excited, too.

Mrs. Mack grinned and called upstairs, "Annie? Could you come down here?"

"I'm in the middle of a report, Mom. Can't it wait?"

"Can't you take a break for a minute!" her mom answered with a laugh. "Come on down. It won't take long."

Annie came downstairs and sat beside Alex on the couch. She glanced at her sister with one eyebrow raised, which in secret sister code meant *What's up with Mom and Dad?*

Alex rolled her eyes and shrugged. Which meant *Haven't got a clue.*

But Alex couldn't wait for her parents' news. As soon as Mr. and Mrs. Mack sat down, she burst out, "I signed up to go on a school trip. I mean, if that's okay. Can I go? Please! Please?"

"Whoa," Mr. Mack said with a chuckle. "What kind of trip?"

Alex remembered Louis's words. "Oh—*very* educational."

"When?" Mrs. Mack asked.

"This weekend."

"This weekend?" Mrs. Mack exclaimed.

"I'm sorry, Alex," Mr. Mack said. "I don't think you can go."

"But why not?" Alex exclaimed. "All my friends are going!"

"If all your friends jumped off the Paradise Valley Chemical building, would you jump, too?" Annie asked.

Alex made a face. "Very funny."

Annie grinned. "Sorry, Alex. I couldn't resist."

"Well, Alex," Mr. Mack explained, "because this is the weekend of our family getaway! Remember?"

George and Barbara Mack exchanged an excited look.

Alex blinked. Weekend getaway? She didn't remember anything about a weekend getaway. What in the world could it be?

"And not a moment too soon," George Mack added. "We need to spend more quality time together as a family."

"But, Dad!" Alex exclaimed. "Can't we spend more quality time some other time?"

"No. The reservations are made." Mr. Mack grinned at his older daughter. "We're off to the dude ranch on Friday night!"

"The *what!?*" Alex and Annie shrieked at once.

Mr. Mack's smile slipped a little. "You remember. The dude ranch. We talked about it months ago. We dress up in cowboy clothes, ride horses, learn how to square-dance. Eat beans and biscuits. Doesn't it sound wonderful?"

"I don't believe this," Alex muttered.

"Now, girls, we've already made the reservations," Mrs. Mack said. "We all spend way too much time indoors at our computers, around the microwave and TV, under artificial light. It can't be good for us."

"Just think," Mr. Mack added. "At the dude ranch, we'll be spending our days out in the sunshine. Sleeping in bunkhouses with the windows thrown wide open. Why, they even have camp sing-alongs around a great big campfire beneath the stars each night. There's supposed to be a meteor shower this weekend. It'll be a wonderful time for us to get in touch with nature *and* be together."

"But, Dad," Annie said. "I have other plans for this weekend."

"And my school trip?" Alex reminded them. "It's a *science* trip, Dad. Explorations with the Science and Nature Club. Mr. Hendricks is the adviser. You're always after me to be more interested in my science schoolwork, Dad. And guess what? I'll get extra credit toward my final grade!"

"Oh."

Mr. and Mrs. Mack looked at each other.

"Well, obviously, I'm delighted you're showing an interest in science, Alex," Mr. Mack said.

"And she could use the extra credit," Mrs. Mack noted.

Alex's parents leaned back thoughtfully.

Alex crossed her fingers. She hated to pop their bubble. But this was important!

The phone rang, and Mrs. Mack answered it.

Annie grabbed Alex by the arm. "Alex, dear, would you help me in the kitchen?"

"Huh?"

"Sodas," Annie said, pulling Alex along behind her. "Let's get everybody something to drink."

Once in the kitchen, Annie got down four glasses and whispered, "Look, Alex. I know your school trip's really important to you. So I'm going to be nice and help you get out of this family thing."

Alex stared at her sister suspiciously. "Uh-huh. Now tell me what you're *really* after."

"Nothing!"

"Annie . . ."

"Um, well, Bryce and I have plans."

Bryce was this guy who worked at the public library. He was the first thing Annie had ever been interested in that didn't fit on a slide under a microscope!

"Anyway," Annie was saying, "he doesn't get that many Saturdays off, so we kind of wanted to spend the whole day together."

Alex grinned. "Got it. Now, what can we do to make sure we get out of this dude ranch thing?"

Annie put her arm around her sister. "Beg?"

Alex grinned. "Plead?"

"Cry!"

"Hold our breath till we both turn blue!"

Alex and Annie burst into giggles. It was just like the old days, Alex thought. She and her big sister, a team in the game of life against the parent team. Trying to get out of chores or wrangle an extra hour before bedtime.

"Seriously, though," Annie said thoughtfully. "I think we should focus on the educational factor."

"Right," Alex agreed. "And remember to look cute and sweet and adorable!"

Annie grinned. "Let's go!"

The girls trooped back into the living room, a united front against authority.

"Dad, I really need to go on this trip," Alex began. "Think how much science stuff I'll learn. And I really, *really* need the extra credit—"

"I agree," her dad said.

"But, Dad, please, you don't understand—"

"Alex!" Mr. Mack chuckled. "I said you're right."

"What? You mean I can go?" Alex asked in surprise.

"No dude ranch?" Annie exclaimed.

"Even better," Mrs. Mack said with a secret smile.

Uh-oh.

Alex looked at Annie. *Now what?*

Annie looked at Alex. *I'm afraid to find out!*

Mr. Mack laughed. "How about if we go, too?"

"We?" Alex's stomach lurched. "Go, too? Where?"

"That was Mr. Hendricks on the telephone," Mr. Mack said. "Your science teacher?"

How could I forget? "Uh-huh."

"Well, Mr. Hendricks was really impressed with how well I hit it off with the kids when I came to talk to your science class last winter. Now, guess what? He's looking for parents to go along on the Science and Nature Club trip. He thought your mother and I would be super chaperons."

Alex opened her mouth, but nothing came out.

"Plus, get this. There are a few more parents going, too, of course, but he's desperate for more. A lot of parents seem too busy this weekend—something about the Paradise Valley bowling team. So, anyway, Mr. Hendricks wondered if you'd go along, too, Annie. You know you always were one of his favorite students. And he felt you'd be a good role model for the younger kids."

Oh, no! Alex thought. *Not Annie, too!*

Annie looked at Alex helplessly.

"But, Dad, it's . . . it's impossible," Annie said. "I've got plans. I—I have things I need to do. . . ."

The phone rang again.

Barbara Mack answered. "Hello? Just a minute. Annie, it's for you." She grinned and whispered, *"Bryce!"*

Annie stood up. "I'll take it in the kitchen."

A few short minutes later, she wandered back into the living room, looking as if she'd just lost her best friend in the world. She flopped down on the couch next to Alex and sighed. "Okay, I'll go."

"Annie!" Alex whispered. "You can't!"

Annie shrugged. "I can. The librarian's cat has a cold or something. So Bryce has to fill in for her this Saturday at the library."

"For the cat?"

"No, silly. For the librarian. So she can look after her cat."

"I didn't even know cats got colds."

"Well, then," Mr. Mack said. "Shall we consider it settled?"

"I'll just go cancel the dude ranch reservations," Mrs. Mack suggested, getting up to find the brochure. "Hey, maybe we can do that later in the summer, hmm?"

"Yeah, Mom. Sure," Alex mumbled. She thought a moment, then tried again. "Dad, are you *sure* you and Mom want to do this? It's definitely *not* going to be any fun."

"Oh, Alex, I think it will be great. It solves all our problems. We'll be getting away from it all. We'll be out in the fresh air. And we'll all be together. Instead of a dude ranch, we'll just go camping. Plus, this will give us a chance to get in touch with what you're doing at school. Get to know your friends better."

"But, Dad! I don't need you to know my friends better!" Alex rolled her eyes.

"Don't worry, Alex," Mrs. Mack said. "We won't do anything to embarrass you. We promise."

Alex sank down into the cushions. She couldn't believe it. *Embarrass me?* This was her worst nightmare.

Her parents were going to chaperon an overnight school trip.

Even worse, her big sister was going, too!

This had to be high on the list of junior high school's top ten most humiliating experiences.

"Yes," Mr. Mack said with a smile. "It's going to be absolutely perfect."

Perfect? Alex thought. *It's going to be perfectly awful!*

CHAPTER 3

Danielle Atron finished the last sip of tea and set her china cup in its saucer on her spotless executive desk.

She touched up her already perfect lipstick, then dabbed her mouth with a tissue.

But the bright red color did nothing to brighten her mood. Neither did the tea. She snapped her silver compact shut, then pressed a button on her interoffice intercom. "I want to see Vince and Dave in my office. Immediately."

She smoothed a slight wrinkle in her skirt as she leaned back in her plush chair to wait. Only moments ago, she'd received a phone call from the corporate bosses who were bankrolling Paradise Valley Chemical—and her precious GC 161 research.

They wanted to see some results—soon. Or, they threatened, they would have to stop all funding. Paradise Valley Chemical would shut down. Hundreds of people would be out of work. And, since it was the major employer in Paradise Valley, the whole town might go under.

But Danielle Atron didn't care about any of that. All she cared about was that she might lose her executive position—and all her hard work would go down the tubes.

Not a chance, she thought. She'd worked long and hard to get where she was. One day soon, she'd be rich and famous. People the world over would scramble to pay any price to get their hands on GC 161—the greatest drug to come along since penicillin. Once perfected, it would allow people to stuff their greedy faces with as much food as they wanted—and never gain a pound.

Getting barked at about GC 161 reminded her of that prickly problem that Vince had repeatedly failed to solve. They still hadn't caught that pesky GC 161 kid!

This kid had become a thorn in Danielle Atron's side. A bad-luck omen that haunted her, jinxing her work. If that kid talked, it could jeopardize the entire project. Maybe even put her behind bars! She shuddered.

If only they could get their hands on this slippery kid!

Then her research and development scientists—led by the brilliant but manageable George Mack—would have a human guinea pig for their experiments.

Danielle Atron was convinced that would quickly lead to success. No one would worry about one kid once her own face hit the cover of *Time* magazine.

She twisted her tissue as if she were wringing someone's neck. *But I have to get my hands on that kid!*

"Excuse me, Ms. Atron," a voice crackled on the intercom. "Vince and Dave are here."

Danielle Atron smiled like a hungry tiger. "Send them in."

The two men appeared in her doorway. Vince

straightened his well-tailored suit and pasted on an obedient smile as he strode confidently into the room.

Dave lifted his blue baseball cap to scratch his head, then, smacking his bubble gum, tugged it back on. Ambling in like a good-natured puppy, he blew a tremendous pink bubble—and popped it.

Danielle Atron cringed.

Vince's arm shot out, blocking Dave's path.

"Wha—?"

Vince pointed to a shiny, spotless waste can by the door. "The gum."

"But, Vince, it's a new piece!"

"Spit!"

Dave hung his head and reluctantly pulled the pink wad from his mouth. "Bombs away!" he called, then dropped it into the can with a loud *plunk.*

"Vince? Remind me," Danielle Atron said with a sarcastic smile. "Just how much are we paying this 'valuable' employee?"

Vince just cleared his throat. "Sorry, Ms. Atron."

"Sit!" she ordered the two men.

They sat. Dave immediately began to twirl the plush leather seat around.

Danielle Atron grimaced.

Vince stared at the ceiling and silently counted to ten.

"Vince," Danielle Atron began. "We have a little problem."

"Yes, Ms. Atron?"

She leaned forward on her desk, her hands clasped so tightly her knuckles were turning white. "My backers are on my back again. They're threatening to pull the plug on the entire GC 161 project unless I show them some results—soon. I've managed to toss them a few bones now and then. Some of George Mack's latest research results kept them happy for a while. But now they're getting—how shall I say?—*impatient.* And I won't lose this project. Do I make myself clear?"

Vince gulped. A tiny bead of sweat trickled down the back of his starched white shirt.

"Let me put it simply, Vince."

Vince leaned forward in his chair. "Yes, Ms. Atron?"

"Find—that—kid."

"We're doing our best, Ms. Atron."

"Vince, I don't think you understand. School will be out soon. Then Paradise Valley kids will scatter. They'll be heading off to summer camp, going on vacation with their parents, running off to pitch hay on Granny's farm . . ."

"My granny had a little farm," Dave said fondly. "But when Paradise Valley Chemical offered her cash for it, she took the money and ran off to Atlantic City to play the slot machines. She never came back." He sniffed sadly. "I miss those little piggies. . . ."

Vince rubbed at his pounding temples as Danielle Atron stood up impatiently.

"My point, gentlemen, is that soon it will be next to impossible to find the GC 161 kid."

Vince nodded. "And that's why we've come up with this plan," he said. "We've collected detailed information on every club meeting, dance, or sporting event left in this school year. If we have to attend every activity on this list, we'll find the GC 161 kid!"

Dave peeked over Vince's shoulder. He read the entry at the top of the list: "Science and Nature Club's Explorations trip."

Take a Hike!

"That's one of the clubs Paradise Valley Chemical sponsors," Vince said loftily. "We're donating the food and the equipment for their trip to Paradise Valley State Park, and we've reserved one of the sites for the club. I know where they'll be, what they'll be doing, and the names, addresses, and phone numbers of every child and adult who'll be on the trip."

"Very efficient, Vince," Danielle Atron said grudgingly. "I assume you're planning to join them."

"Oooh! That sounds like fun!" Dave exclaimed. "I've always loved camping at the state park, ever since I started watching Yogi Bear cartoons."

Vince rolled his eyes.

"Enough of this foolish chitchat!" Danielle Atron returned to her seat and opened a folder. "Goodbye, gentlemen. I look forward to your successful report. And Vince?"

"Yes, Ms. Atron?"

"Let's make it soon?"

"Yes, Ms. Atron," Vince said, bowing slightly as he rose. Then he turned and hustled Dave out of the office.

Vince had almost convinced himself that this problem with the GC 161 kid would maybe, just maybe, fade away. After all, it had been a long time since the accident. The kid, whoever he was, hadn't gone to the cops. He hadn't shown up in intensive care at the hospital. And he hadn't tried to get rich by selling his story to some reporter.

Well, obviously the problem wasn't going to disappear. And time was running out. No way was he going to let Dave's dumb driving accident or some mutant kid ruin his career at Paradise Valley Chemical.

The sooner he found that kid, the better.

"Time to get packing," Vince told Dave as he strode down the hallway. "We're going to scrounge up every gizmo, detector, and device we can get our hands on from the guys in the lab."

"How about marshmallows?" Dave asked. "Are you gonna bring 'em? Or shall I?"

Vince clenched his teeth.

That was another big plus, Vince thought. Once he found that GC 161 kid, he could quit hanging out with Dave.

Heads up, kid! Vince thought with a nasty grin. *I'm gonna nail you if it's the last thing I ever do.*

Across town, at Danielle Atron Junior High School, Alex and Ray wandered into Mr. Hendricks's class for the Science and Nature Club meeting. "This is the oddest mix of kids I've ever seen in one room," Alex whispered to Ray.

There were kids dressed like they had bought new clothes from the mall. And those who looked like models for a camping catalogue. There were science nerds. Even a couple of kids in black leather jeans and heavy-metal T-shirts.

Alex and Ray sat down in two vacant seats right behind Scott.

Scott turned around in his seat and propped his chin on his folded arms. "Hey, Alex. I hear your parents are going on the trip as chaperons. That's great."

"Yeah." Alex forced a smile. "Great."

"I really enjoyed that nature hike I went on with your dad last fall," he added. "He's a nice guy."

"Thanks." Why did it feel so weird for the

43

cool guy you liked to like your geeky dad? Alex wondered.

Just then, Kelly showed up and spotted Alex and Scott talking.

She hurried over, but a kid with broken glasses taped at the bridge was sitting in the seat next to Scott. "Oh, Norman," Kelly sang in her sweetest voice. "Would you mind terribly if I sat here!"

"Uh, no," Norman croaked, his voice cracking. He pushed his glasses up on his nose, stuffed his ballpoint pen in the pocket protector of his white shirt, and got up. "Not at all."

"Thank you," Kelly said as she slid into his seat. There was that beauty queen smile again. "Hi, Scott. Hi, Alex." She gave Alex a look. "Nice hat. Unusual color."

Alex tugged at her fuchsia denim hat. "Thanks." How come Kelly's compliments always felt like insults?

"Oh, Scott," Kelly said. "Do you have a minute? You're so good at math. And I really need some help with tonight's homework. Problem number six?"

"Sure, Kelly." Scott turned around to pull his math book out of his pack.

Kelly grinned over her shoulder at Alex. " 'Scuse us." Then she flipped her long brown hair over her shoulder and turned her back on Alex.

Alex made a face at the back of Kelly's head.

I must be totally nuts, Alex thought. Her fantasy getaway adventure had turned into *Nightmare on Elm Street*.

The guest list included her parents. Her sister, Annie. Her science teacher, Mr. Hendricks (who adored her sister, Annie). And Kelly, her least favorite person in the world.

This trip was turning out to be the worst idea of the century. Maybe she should just invite Vince and Dave to come along, too!

CHAPTER 4

"Isn't this fun?" George Mack said cheerfully Friday after school.

Nobody answered.

Alex winced. Did her father *have* to be so cheery? "Dad! It's raining."

Alex glanced around her at the students and parent chaperons waiting for the school activity bus to take them to the park. Everybody looked pretty bummed out by the rain.

And the activity bus was late.

"See?" Robyn moaned. "I told you. Me and the outdoors—not a happy combination."

"Hey, this is part of the fun," George Mack insisted. "Getting close to nature. Dealing with her whims without the artificial comforts of modern civilization. Think of it as a challenge. An adventure."

Even a few of the other parents glared at that.

"George," Barbara Mack whispered, gently taking her husband's arm. "Maybe we should just wait quietly."

Finally the bus arrived. The kids crushed on to get good seats. Alex and Ray wound up sitting near the back behind Scott and Kelly.

Lucky for Alex, her parents and Annie sat up front with the other chaperons.

But her luck wasn't going to hold. Ten minutes after the bus drove off, her dad stood up and smiled back at all the passengers. He waved, gave a cheery thumbs-up, and sat back down.

Uh-oh. Alex glared at Ray. "I have a feeling I'm never going to forgive you for suggesting this trip in the first place."

Ray just grinned sheepishly.

"I've got an idea!" Mr. Pines exclaimed. His daughter, Penny, slunk down in her seat with a groan. "Let's sing camp songs! It'll cheer us all up and make the trip go faster. Let's see now. Oh—I've got one." He cleared his throat. " 'I've been working on the railroad, all the live-long day'—Come on, everybody!"

Mr. Mack and a few of the adults joined in. Ouch! Somebody was really off-key.

Some of the kids laughed.

Some sang along, but in goofy voices.

Behind her, Alex heard Louis making up fake words: "I've been working on Hendricks's science test, all the live-long day...."

Ray snickered.

But Alex cringed and sank down in her seat. *Oh, Dad! How could you? Singing dopey camp songs is so totally out of it!*

Suddenly Alex's face began to feel funny as a hot blush crept up her neck.

She used to blush like a neon sign, flashing her emotions uncensored to the entire world. That was bad enough. But her GC 161 shower had changed all that. Now, whenever she got really nervous or embarrassed, she glowed. Not the pretty pink glow of lovely girls in old-fashioned novels, but a weird, throbbing, toxic-looking golden glow that made her look like an alien from Planet Firefly.

"Alex! You're glowing!" Ray whispered worriedly. "Get down!"

Alex ducked down in her seat. She yanked the hood of her green rain poncho up over her head and pressed her hot cheeks to the cool glass of the window. She hated this! It was the worst side effect of her whole GC 161 ordeal. Her other powers could at least be fun sometimes, and with Annie's help she had learned over the months to manage them pretty well. But this neon blush thing was almost impossible to control!

Counting backward sometimes helped. "One hundred, ninety-nine, ninety-eight . . ."

In the next seat back, Louis called out, "Hey, Mr. Mack! Alex wants to sing 'Ninety-nine Bottles of Beer on the Wall!' "

"That's a good one!" Alex heard her dad say. "But this is a school trip. Maybe we should say 'soda'! Come on, everybody. 'Ninety-nine bottles of soda on the wall, ninety-nine bottles of soda . . .' "

How mortifying! Now Alex's face throbbed! She ducked down below the seat, pretending to look for something in her backpack.

"Alex! Are you okay?" Kelly looked over her seat back. "My seat is being bumped."

Alex kept her face to the ground. "Fine!" she squeaked.

"What's wrong with Alex?" Robyn asked from across the aisle. "Is she carsick?"

"She's fine!" Ray repeated, trying to distract everybody. "Really. Just turn around. Sing! 'Eighty-six bottles of soda on the wall . . . '"

Kelly frowned at Ray, then turned back in her seat. Robyn turned back to her conversation with Nicole.

"Alex?" Ray whispered. "Let me see. Hey, I think it's fading. Here, try a sip of water from my canteen. It's ice cold."

Alex took a sip, took a deep breath, then winced as she heard her dad's lone voice begin verse seventy-two, singing in time to the clunking windshield wipers. If her dad didn't stop singing, she was going to have to spend the entire trip on the floor.

Eventually, the bus chugged past a sign that read PARADISE VALLEY STATE PARK. The rain tapered off to a light drizzle as they drove deeper into the woods. At last the bus stopped at their assigned campground.

Alex and her friends pressed their faces to the glass.

She saw a huge clearing in the trees. In the middle, dozens of large rocks encircled a dugout for a campfire. Nearby was a covered shelter with a cement floor and several picnic tables. Off in the distance, she spotted a small wooden building—probably the bathrooms.

That was all.

Except for a wooden sign stuck into the ground with the site number, "13."

"Good omen," Robyn remarked.

One by one the chaperons and students descended from the bus. Mr. Hendricks ran over to open the bus's luggage compartment. "George, would you help me with these?" he said as he began to lug out huge duffel-looking things.

"Okay, everybody," Mr. Hendricks called out. He took off his glasses to wipe off the rain. "Divide up into groups of four. Then grab a tent and set it up. Be sure to use the rain flap. Looks like it's going to rain the rest of the night."

"You mean we have to set these things up

ourselves?" Robyn said. "Nobody told me about this part!"

Alex grabbed a tent to share with Robyn and Nicole.

"I'd better sleep with you guys," Annie said as she grabbed the other end.

"But, Annie, shouldn't you sleep with the other chaperons?"

"I don't think so, Alex. Besides"—she lowered her voice—"you might need me. You know. If anything . . . 'weird' happens?"

"Something weird already did happen," Alex whispered back. "I came on this trip with you and Mom and Dad!"

The two sisters dragged the tent over to a spot that looked pretty good.

"How about right here?" Robyn said dryly. "In this nice puddle."

"Don't worry, Robyn," Nicole assured her. "The tent's pretty waterproof. Here. Grab this pole."

Putting up the tent was not so easy, they soon found out. How were they supposed to know what poles went where?

"Hey, girls!" Louis shouted over. "Watch the

experts!" He and Ray were putting up their tent with the help of Norman, the kid with the taped-up glasses.

Nicole put her hands on her hips. "Hey, are we going to let the guys outdo us?"

"No way!" Alex cheered. "Come on, Annie. Turn on that brainpower of yours and help us figure this out!"

"I'm trying!" Annie insisted.

With a good attitude and plenty of teamwork, it only took them three or four tries to get the tent set up. Inside, it was pretty dry, if not very roomy, and tall enough for the four of them to stand up inside.

Alex was surprised. "This is neat. Kind of like a clubhouse or something."

"Alex! Robyn!" They heard Ray yelling. "Check it out."

The girls stepped outside to look.

"Ta-da!" Ray swung his arm toward his tent.

Alex and her friends stared skeptically. The tent had kind of an odd shape to it.

"I think maybe you've got a long and a short pole mixed up or something," Alex suggested.

"Hey," Ray said, pretending his feelings

were hurt. "It's our own design." He stuck his nose in the air, and he and his tentmates went inside.

"Slam!" Louis said, pretending to slam a door in their faces.

Alex giggled. She looked around in the dark drizzle.

Should she or shouldn't she?

She couldn't resist—she loved to tease Ray. No one would see her out here.

Turning sideways a little, she wiggled her forefinger, aiming it for one of the main tent poles.

Seconds later the guys' whole tent fell down on top of them.

"Hey!" the guys shouted.

Alex and her friends burst out laughing.

Annie crept up behind her. "Alex!" she whispered. "Was that you?"

"Oops!" Alex giggled. "Sorry, Annie. I couldn't help it. But nobody saw me."

Annie shook her head. "Probably not. But you'd better be careful out here."

"I will be," Alex said.

Ray, Louis, and Newman emerged from their tent.

"Need some help?" Alex asked them.

"Sure," Ray said. "Not that it's really necessary ..."

In minutes the tent was set up, and the guys threw their bags inside.

"I'm starving. How about pizza?" Louis suggested.

"Louis, I don't think they deliver to the wilderness," Robyn commented.

"Really?" Louis shook his head. "I thought you could get pizza delivered anywhere."

The kids walked over to the shelter. Mr. Mack and Mr. Hendricks were cooking hot dogs on a nearby grill, while Mrs. Mack held a large black umbrella over them. Several students milled around, holding paper plates.

"More hot dogs'll be coming off the grill in just a minute!" George Mack called out cheerfully. "Grab a plate!"

"Is your dad always this cheerful?" Scott asked Alex.

"Believe it or not," Alex said, "most of the time."

"I admire his attitude," Scott added.

"Oh, Scott!" Kelly sang out. "Over here! I saved you a place!"

"Come on, guys," Scott said to Alex and her friends. "Let's sit over here."

Kelly made a face.

I guess she doesn't like sitting with a bunch of eighth-graders, Alex thought.

After a quick supper of hot dogs, chips, and soda, Mr. Hendricks went over a few rules and plans for the next day. "I guess we'd better turn in soon," he suggested. "We've got a big day planned tomorrow."

The adults stayed up to talk awhile. But most of the kids headed off to bed.

What else is there to do in the dark and drizzle? Alex wondered.

Alex crawled into her tent with Annie and her friends. There was just enough room for the four of them to lay out their sleeping bags like sardines in a can: Nicole, Robyn, Alex, then Annie.

Alex could hear voices and scattered giggling throughout the camp as everyone settled down for the night.

Annie went straight to sleep. Alex and her two friends talked softly for a while, then Nicole's voice faded, and Robyn conked out, too.

Alex curled down into her sleeping bag. She was warm enough, but the ground was pretty hard. Yawning, she thought, *We ought to be getting double extra credit for this trip.*

"Pssst! Alex! Wake up!"

Still half asleep, Alex sat up on one elbow and looked around. "Wha—"

Uh-oh!

A flashlight, a hiking boot, a granola bar, and Alex's purple toothbrush, which had been floating around the tent like miniature planets in a solar system science project, fell to the ground with a few muffled thuds.

"Oh, no, not again!" Alex shook her head to try to clear it.

This happened at home sometimes, when she had crazy dreams. But usually, of course, it happened in the privacy of her own bedroom, with no one but Annie around to see it.

Alex felt her face glowing again.

"Hey, Alex," Robyn mumbled as she turned over in her sleep. "Would you please turn off your flashlight?"

"Alex, do something!" Annie whispered.

"I'm trying!" Alex covered her face with a towel and concentrated on clearing her mind.

She peeked out from under the towel at her two friends.

Nicole slept like a log. Robyn was snoring.

Whew! That was close, Alex thought.

Crunch, crunch.

Alex grabbed Annie's arm. "Did you hear that?"

"What?"

"That rustling sound—outside!"

Alex and Annie listened closely.

Something with big feet was stomping toward their tent.

Alex held her breath. *No bears*, she told herself. Nicole promised her there were *no bears* in Paradise Valley State Park. . . .

Suddenly a big shape loomed in front of the tent. Something scratched on the nylon tent.

Alex and Annie grabbed each other.

"Who's there?" Annie bravely called out.

"Is everything okay in there?"

Alex let out the breath she'd been holding in one big gush. Those big feet belonged to the beauty queen.

"Kelly!" Annie whispered in her best junior chaperon voice. "What are you doing up wandering around?" She shone her flashlight in Kelly's face.

"I was, um, in the bath house flossing my teeth." She peeked in through the tiny unzipped part of the tent. "I saw lights in your tent, Alex. And weird shadows. Like things were flying around. What's going on?"

Annie blocked Kelly's view. "Everything's fine," she reassured her. "Alex and I were just ... just making hand shadows with our flashlights."

"Yeah," Alex put in. "Annie does a great bunny."

"Oh. How ... cute." Kelly smiled. "Well, then. See you in the morning."

Annie zipped up the tent flap all the way. Then she turned to her sister.

"Alex! You're going to have to be more careful with your powers!" She kept her voice low so they wouldn't wake up Robyn and Nicole. But to Alex, it still sounded like getting yelled at. "Any slip-up is going to show up even more out here in the woods."

"Okay, Annie. I didn't do any of this on purpose. But I'll try extra hard. I promise."

Alex scooped her things back into her pack, then snuggled way down in her sleeping bag and tucked her face down in her covers. She'd have to be really careful. The last thing she needed was a snoopy Kelly getting suspicious about her powers. Especially since Kelly didn't like her much anyway. *She'd probably turn me in just for fun*, Alex thought.

"At least we don't have to worry about Vince and Dave looking for us out here," Alex whispered.

Alex and Annie giggled.

"Yeah," Annie whispered back. "Vince is definitely not the outdoor type."

Not far from the campsite Vince and Dave drove a company four-wheeler into Paradise Valley State Park, trying to find their way in the light drizzle. Fogged-up windows made it hard to see. Vince was steamed, too. But not just because of the weather.

Vince wore a disguise—a rather good one, he thought. A lot of the kids in Paradise Valley knew what he and Dave looked like, so they had to be careful when they conducted one of their search missions for Ms. Atron.

Tonight Vince looked like somebody's rumpled old dad out for a weekend of fishing: He wore an old plain shirt and wrinkled khaki pants (which he'd normally never be caught dead in), a fishing vest, a crumpled white fishing hat, and a black wig and fake beard. Actually, he thought he looked rather handsome— in a tacky sort of way. He'd even brought along a fly rod, a tackle box, and one of those basket things you put fish in.

Vince's own mother wouldn't recognize him. *If she were still talking to me,* he thought with a harsh chuckle.

But Dave . . . what was he going to do about Dave?

Dave popped a fluffy marshmallow into his mouth and chewed. "I still don't understand why you're so mad at me, Vince."

Vince rolled his eyes. "When I told you to wear a disguise, Dave, I was expecting something a *little* more subtle."

Dave looked down at himself. "This is subtle."

"Subtle?" Vince nearly shrieked. "You call a smelly old, moth-eaten *bear costume* subtle?"

"Sure!" Dave insisted. "I'll blend right in with nature—and all the other little creatures in the forest."

"Dave, you look like a leftover from a bad Halloween party," Vince muttered. "Besides, you're going to look ridiculous if anybody sees you, because there are no bears in Paradise Valley."

"No bears?" Dave exclaimed. "I thought all state parks had bears."

"That's only in cartoons, idiot."

Dave hugged his marshmallow bag and turned toward the window with a pout. "Maybe they're just all hiding from *you.*"

Vince gripped the steering wheel and bit back a reply.

Got to find that kid, Vince told himself. *I don't know how much longer I can put up with this guy.*

CHAPTER 5

"Rise and shine!"

A groggy Alex peeked out the tent flaps.

"Good morning, Alex!" Mr. Hendricks called out cheerfully. He blew on a small ear-splitting whistle as he marched around the campsite waking students.

Alex covered her ears.

Nicole bolted upright. "What in the world—?"

"It's Mr. Hendricks," Alex told her. "I think we need to find him a Cub Scout troop!"

"What time is it, anyway?" Annie asked, sitting up.

"Too early!" Robyn mumbled without moving.

"I thought this trip was supposed to be about relaxing with nature," Alex grumbled. "Taking a break. Rest!"

"Wrong trip, Alex," Nicole teased. "This trip's about getting up early and tackling nature."

"Wake me up when breakfast's ready," Robyn mumbled through her sleeping bag.

"Forget it, Robyn." Nicole stood up and stretched. "Out in the wilderness, if you don't help make breakfast, you don't eat breakfast."

Robyn sat up with her eyes closed. "Got it."

Alex dressed quickly in jeans, a T-shirt with a blue flannel shirt on top, and hiking boots. Then she ran a brush through her hair, tugged on a baseball cap, and stepped outside. Some of the kids were straggling out of their tents. There was no movement at all around Ray and Louis's tent. *Dead to the world*, Alex guessed with a chuckle. No sign of Kelly, either.

Alex stretched and breathed in. The air was cool and tinged with the smell of woodsmoke. The sun shone through the few remaining clouds. It was going to be a beautiful day.

She glanced over at the circle of stones. Scott

was not only up and awake, but he had a nice fire going.

Alex wandered over and sat down on a rock. " 'Morning."

"Oh, hi, Alex." Scott grinned. "How'd you sleep?"

Alex shrugged. "Pretty good," she admitted with a smile. "But it's kind of early for a Saturday!"

"Here—have some hot chocolate." Using an old red oven mitt, he carefully lifted a blue enamel coffeepot off the fire and poured hot water into a mug of cocoa mix. Alex saw another pot and smelled coffee. He'd even perked some java for the grown-ups!

Alex blew on her hot chocolate and warmed her hands on the mug. "Thanks."

Scott nodded and took a sip from his own mug. "Best part of the day, before everybody else is up and about. Don't you think?"

"Uh, sure!" Alex said, crossing the fingers of one hand behind her back. But looking around, Alex had to admit that maybe he was right. It was nice sitting here in the morning quiet, watching the mist rise off the trees.

Alex laughed when she saw her parents crawl out of their tent. Her mom's hair was a wreck, and she still looked half asleep. Her dad groaned and stretched.

"Mr. and Mrs. Mack," Scott called out. "Come have some coffee."

Mr. Mack took a mug of coffee from Scott and grinned. "I think the ground's a lot harder than it used to be when we went camping years ago."

Mrs. Mack yawned. "We're just out of practice, George."

"I'm glad it's clearing up. We should see quite a meteor show tonight!" Mr. Mack was grinning with excitement.

Mrs. Mack and Alex exchanged a smile.

"Want to help make breakfast, Alex?" Scott asked as he opened a cooler of supplies and handed her a bowl.

"Sure. What are we making?"

"About three hundred pancakes."

"Scott, I think we need a bigger bowl."

Not far away the door to an abandoned miner's cabin slammed open.

Vince the fisherman and Dave the bear stepped out on the small front porch.

"Ah! Smell that fresh air," Dave cried, thumping his furry chest with his fists.

Vince broke out in a coughing fit.

Dave pounded him on the back. "Vince! Are you okay?"

Vince threw up his arms. "Yes, I'm fine. *Cough, cough.* There's enough pollen out here to choke an elephant," he muttered.

He led Dave to the van parked around back. It had been too dark and rainy the night before to unload and set up all their electronic gear.

"Well, don't just stand there," Vince said, sneering at Dave's cuddly costume. "Unload this stuff. We've got a lot of setting up to do."

Dave reached in and grabbed a huge box of electronic gizmos: walkie-talkies, binoculars, short-wave radios, and an assortment of GC 161 detectors.

"What are we going to do with all of this, Vince?" Dave asked as he headed for the cabin.

Vince opened the cabin door for Dave. "We're going to set up a kind of command center in here. Then we'll set up these tiny detectors at various marked points along the trails."

"How do we know where to put them?"

"I have precise information on where these kids will be all day," Vince explained. He tacked up a park map on the rough wooden wall. "The Science and Nature Club group will be hiking in this area," he said, outlining it in thick red marker. "See these lines? They're hiking trails. And all the trails in this section are marked with circles: yellow, green, white, orange, and the ever popular *red*."

Vince chuckled as he began to unload the box of devices. "These tiny devices are like security beepers in department stores."

"The ones that catch shoplifters?" Dave asked.

"Exactly. Only these are high-tech. That's why they're so tiny. We'll plant these along the trail, wait for our little GC 161 kid to hike past, and *wham!*" He slammed his fist down on the rough wooden table.

Dave yelped.

"We nab our little guinea pig, cage him up, and deliver him to to Ms. Atron."

Dave gulped. "We aren't gonna hurt him, are we?"

Vince smiled like a fox. "Of course not. Ms. Atron likes her lab rats alive and kicking when the research guys start their experiments."

CHAPTER 6

After breakfast Mr. Hendricks gave the Danielle Atron Junior High School Science and Nature Club a lecture on the native plants, animals, and rocks in the Paradise Valley area. Then he gave everyone a handout sheet.

"This afternoon we'll split up into small groups of about eight students—with a chaperon, of course," Mr. Hendricks explained. "Each group will hike a different trail. Your project is to identify and photograph as many items on this list as possible. You may take small samples, but please don't pick anything that's growing or otherwise disturb nature as you find it."

Alex stared at her copy of the list. Wow! It was long!

"See, what'd I tell you?" she whispered to Ray. "More schoolwork!"

Ray and Louis looked over the list and gulped.

"I don't guess we'll have much hammock time," Louis said.

"When we return home," Mr. Hendricks went on, "your group's photos and observations will be put together in a group project. Your extra credit will be based on your group's report."

Then Mr. Hendricks very quickly counted off the kids into groups, based on where they were sitting.

Alex was delighted as her group was called out: her, Ray, Louis, Robyn, Nicole, Scott, and Norman.

"Let's see," Mr. Hendricks said. "Annie, we'll let you be this group's chaperon. So we need one more student for your group. . . ."

Kelly's hand shot up. "Mr. Hendricks! Me, please?"

Mr. Hendricks smiled. "Fine, Kelly. Next group—"

Alex's face fell.

"Too bad, Alex," Robyn said, patting her on the shoulder. "You can't fight destiny."

After that Mr. Mack volunteered to be Mr. Hendricks's guinea pig while he demonstrated some basic safety and first-aid information.

Mr. Pines led a workshop in tying a variety of special knots.

After lunch the students divided up into their groups.

"I'm really sorry your mother and I won't be hiking along with your group," Mr. Mack told Alex. "Mr. Hendricks assigned your mother and me to command post duty. That means we stick around camp. But at least you and Annie get to hike in the same group. And we'll have some free time right before dinner. Maybe we can all do something together then. Okay?"

"Sure, Dad," Alex said. Her father was smiling. But when she looked closely, she realized how bummed out he really was. Like a puppy who didn't get to follow his kids to school.

That made Alex feel bad. All she'd been thinking about was how geeky her dad could be. But most of the kids didn't seem to notice. And he'd really had his heart set on this family togeth-erness thing.

"Don't forget," Alex added, "there's always tomorrow. Tubing on the river?"

"That does sound like fun," Mr. Mack agreed.

"Besides," Alex added, "you and Mom have been so exhausted lately. Now you'll get a chance just to hang out together at camp—just the two of you. With no phones and nothing to do."

George Mack brightened. "You're right! Thanks for reminding me, Alex. Have fun!"

Alex's group sat down outside her tent to get organized.

"Okay," Annie said. "We need to assign a few jobs before we start. Scott, I'm just along as an adviser. But you've done an Explorations trip be-fore. Why don't you be group leader?"

"Well, I am pretty familiar with the trails out here. I'll be glad to do it—if that's okay with everybody else." He looked around. Everybody nodded.

Alex wasn't surprised. Kids really did seem to like him.

"Great," Annie said. "Then I officially turn

this group over to you." Alex thought she looked relieved.

"Thanks," Scott said. "Okay, then. I guess it's volunteer time." He held up a red spiral notebook. "First, we need somebody to take notes."

Kelly reached for the notebook. "I'll take notes." She smiled and added, "I've been told I have very neat handwriting."

"Oh, great," Robyn whispered to Alex. "It'll be the first time in scientific history that research notes were written with curly letters and little hearts dotting all the *i*'s."

"Shhh!" Alex said with a giggle

But wasn't it funny, Alex thought. Kelly had said almost the same thing that Scott had— speaking up about a talent that made her good for a job. But Scott had sounded modest, honest. Kelly just sounded conceited.

"Next, we need somebody to handle the camera." Scott held up one of those automatic-everything 35mm cameras and grinned. "Compliments of Danielle Atron and Paradise Valley Chemical." He looked around the group.

"How about you, Alex?"

"Me?"

Scott handed her the nifty camera. "Sure."

Alex waved the camera away. "I don't know, Scott. I might mess up the pictures."

"Come on, Alex," Kelly piped in. *"Anybody* could do it."

Thanks a lot, Kelly! Alex thought. Taking the photos for the whole project was a pretty important job. But it gave her confidence that Scott would even think to ask her. "Okay."

The group quickly divided up the rest of the tasks.

Nicole volunteered herself and Robyn to look things up in their paperback nature guides.

Norman volunteered to carry the granola bars, crackers, and juice.

"And we'll bag up any collectible specimens," Ray said, pointing to himself and Louis. "What do we use?"

Annie handed him a box of plastic bags. "Bag each item separately. Label it with name, date, and location where found. And keep all the bags in this totebag."

Ray and Louis stood up with their arms across each other's shoulders.

"Alvarado and Driscoll—"

"That's Driscoll and Alvarado," Louis interrupted.

"At your service," they said together. "You can count on us."

"Okay, guys," Annie said, zipping up her pack. "Has everybody got on sunscreen?"

"Sunscreen?" Louis stared at the sky. He switched to his best TV weather guy voice: "But, Annie, it's still partly cloudy."

"Believe me," Annie said, "you can still get sunburned when it's cloudy. Besides, I think it's clearing up."

So everybody took a moment to slather on sunscreen.

"Want to try some of mine?" Kelly asked the girls. "It's from the makeup counter at Dalton's. You wouldn't believe how much it cost," she bragged. "But it smells wonderful!" She held out her arm.

"I can't smell anything," Robyn whined. "My nose is stopped up. I guess my allergies are already kicking in."

Alex and Nicole sniffed.

"Whoaaa!" Nicole said. "Smells good enough to eat!"

"Smells like honey and coconut," Alex agreed.

Robyn rubbed her nose. "Hope those bears don't smell you."

"Bears!" Kelly squeaked. "Did you say bears?"

"Kelly, there are no—*ow!*"

Alex jabbed Nicole in the ribs.

Nicole frowned a question, which Alex answered with a mischievous wink.

"No what?" Kelly demanded.

"Uh, no . . . no sunscreens in the world that smell as good as yours," she thought up quickly.

Alex could tell that made Kelly nervous.

Unfortunately, that just made her stick closer to Scott.

"Okay, guys!" Scott shrugged into the straps of his backpack. "I guess it's time to take a hike!"

The students and Annie followed Scott down the road till he stopped next to a tree marked with a rough red circle of paint the size of a dinner plate.

"These are the trail blazes," Scott said.

"Trail blaze? Like what the pioneers did?" Norman asked.

"Well, sort of. The park people who created

the trail put it there to mark the path." He peered down the trail, then pointed. "You see the next one—way down there on that tree next to the big rock? That's how we can tell we're still on the right trail."

Annie rolled her eyes. "The right trail," she groaned. "And to think I could be spending the day with Bryce." She shifted her pack and started off on the trail. "I think I hate cats...."

"Anybody want a snack?" Norman asked, trailing behind Annie, as he peeled one open for himself.

"Come on, guys." Nicole locked arms with Alex and Robyn. "Follow me."

Not long into the hike, Alex's Red Team actually settled down into a quiet, steady hiking pace. Gradually, the chatter died down.

Scott kept them walking steadily. "The trick for a long hike is pacing," he explained. "Keep your steps short and equally measured."

Alex tried it. She found that it did help her to keep from getting winded.

Alex was surprised. The morning science lecture by Mr. Hendricks had been about as exciting as school. But being out on the trail was fun.

Especially now that the sun was shining. She realized she hadn't thought about the chemical plant in a while. *What a difference!* She could actually feel herself relaxing.

"When do we get to turn around?" Robyn wondered.

"Turn around?" Nicole exclaimed. "You're nuts, Robyn. This is wonderful. I could hike all day. How about you, Alex?"

"I don't know about all day!" Alex said. "But I am having fun."

With nine of them to look, they quickly found a lot of the items on the list. Alex had to admit, she was proud of her sister. It was kind of like having a CD-ROM encyclopedia at your fingertips. Only Annie was a little more fun.

Vince gritted his teeth and glared through his binoculars. Nothing. Not a soul in sight.

Wrapped around the tree branch beside him, Dave growled.

"Must you?" Vince asked with a sign. "This bear act is really getting tiresome."

"It wasn't me growling," Dave said. "It's my stomach. I'm starving. We didn't eat lunch, and all the marshmallows are gone. Can't we take a break? It's almost dinnertime." He peeked at the ground with one eye. "I'm scared of heights, too."

"All right, all right." Vince tucked his binoculars in his shirt and climbed down out of the tree.

Dave climbed halfway down, then tumbled the rest of the way.

After picking up his gear, Vince strolled toward a nice spot on the bank of a small stream and sat down. Then he opened his tackle box and pulled out some sandwiches, some fruit, and two bottles of iced tea.

"Vince!" Dave accused. "You've been holding out on me."

"I had to hide them," Vince explained patiently, the way a parent might speak to a young child. "Otherwise, you'd have eaten them already—and we wouldn't have any dinner now."

"Oh. That makes sense." Dave bit into his sandwich. "Mmm. These are good! Thanks, Vince."

Vince polished off his own sandwich, ignoring Dave's mindless chatter. Then he lay back on the bank with his hat over his face. The gurgling stream was like a gentle lullabye, and soon Vince drifted off to sleep.

Dave peeked at his coworker. "Vince," he called softly. "Oh, Vi-ince!"

No answer. Vince was definitely in dreamland.

Dave very carefully leaned all the way across Vince's sleeping body and quietly opened the tackle box. He sneaked another sandwich out and quickly gobbled it down. Then he couldn't resist. He quietly picked up Vince's fly rod for a quick few minutes of fishing.

I don't know why Vince is always so cranky, Dave thought as he cast his line into the stream. *This is fun! Hunting for that GC 161 kid is the best job I've ever had!*

"Scott! Wait! Don't move!"

Scott had paused on the trail for a drink from his water bottle. Now he froze. "What?"

Alex pointed toward the toe of his scuffed hiking boot.

A tiny multicolored lizard stood not three inches from his foot.

"I don't believe it," Alex barely whispered.

Slowly, slowly, she raised her camera. She turned off the automatic flash. Then she pressed the button.

A tiny *snap!*

The creature moved a few inches, then froze.

Alex motioned to Scott to put his hand down—slowly—next to the tiny creature. That would help show the scale of the lizard. He followed her instructions, so gently the creature didn't move.

Scott looked up at Alex and grinned.

Wouldn't she love a shot of that!

But instead, Alex used the camera's optional zoom to move in close, framing the shot. *Don't move, don't move!* she begged silently. She held the camera steady. She held her breath.

Snap!

The lizard darted into the leaves.

"Did you get it?" Scott asked eagerly.

Alex grinned. "I think so. It'll be great for the report."

Most of the others had gone on ahead a bit. But now Kelly backtracked to find Scott. "What are you two up to?" she demanded, a little too cheerfully and a little too loudly.

Alex was glad she hadn't been around a moment ago.

"Hey, quiet, Kelly," Scott said good-naturedly. "You'll scare all the wildlife away."

"Oh, really?" At first she looked mad. But then she smoothed her face into a pout. "How about walking with me for a while?"

"Sure." He turned back to Alex. "Great shot, Alex. I can't wait to see your pictures when we get back."

Alex watched him walk away with Kelly.

Every few feet he stopped to look at something. Kelly didn't seem interested. She mostly just stood around tapping her foot and waiting.

"Hey, Alex. Look at this!"

Alex jogged up the trail and knelt down to see what Ray had found.

But she never got to see it.

A scream tore through the late-afternoon quiet.

A girl's scream.

Alex jumped to her feet. "It's Robyn!"

CHAPTER 7

Alex and Ray raced off the trail, into the woods toward the scream, as if they were competing at a track meet. The other kids followed close behind them.

"Robyn? Oh, where is she?" Annie said. "She shouldn't have wandered off the trail. Robyn!"

They found her nearby, running around in circles with a long thick stick slung over her shoulder like a baseball bat. And she looked terrified.

Ray and Alex reached her first.

Ray put his arm around her.

Alex's eyes were worried. "Robyn, are you all right?"

For a moment Robyn couldn't speak. Then she stuttered, "I-I saw a b-b-bear!"

The kids glanced nervously at one another. Was this for real?

"Now, Robyn," Nicole began.

"No, Nicole. Really! I *did!*" Robyn insisted. "And that's not all."

"Two bears?" Louis joked. "Or maybe three— with a cute little blond girl named Goldilocks?"

Norman snorted with laughter and pushed his taped glasses up on his nose. "I wish I could have seen that!"

"I'm serious, Louis!" Robyn insisted with a frown. "And guess what? He was leaning over a fisherman lying on the ground. And I think—"

"What? *What!*" everyone shouted.

"I think the fisherman's d-d-dead!"

Everybody started talking at once.

"You're kidding!"

"Are you serious?"

"No way!"

"I don't know," Scott said. "I really find it hard to believe that there are any bears out here."

84

"I agree with Scott," Nicole spoke up. "Now, Robyn, we all know our eyes can play tricks on us out here in the woods. Maybe you just saw—"

"No!" Robyn insisted. "I *saw* a *bear*—"

"Come on, Scott," Kelly whined, pulling on his sleeve. "Let's get out of here."

"And," Robyn added, "the b-bear was fishing."

Norman took a bite of his third granola bar. "That's only natural, you know. It's springtime. Bears wake up out of hibernation pretty hungry. And their huge paws make excellent tools for trout fishing in streams. They just scoop 'em—"

"N-no!" Robyn stuttered. "You don't understand. He was fishing with the dead man's fly rod!"

Alex and her friends stared at Robyn.

Then they all burst out laughing.

"Oh, man, Robyn," Ray choked out. "You really got us with that one."

Louis shook his head in admiration. "I never would have figured you for the practical joke type, Robyn. Give me five!"

"I'm not kidding!" Robyn cried, angry now. "I really saw a bear. And he was really fishing!"

"Give it up, Robyn," Ray said.

Robyn stomped her foot. "I'll prove it. Come on!" With that, she headed off in the opposite direction.

Ray and Louis were quick to follow.

"I gotta see this," Louis joked.

"Hey, Alex—get your camera ready," Ray called back. "This will be great for the report!"

"Oh, brother." Nicole looked at Alex. "Come on, let's go get her before she gets herself lost."

"You don't suppose she really saw a bear, do you?" Alex asked.

"No way," Nicole said.

"Not likely," Scott said.

Annie was trying to get everybody back on the trail. "I really think we should stay on marked paths, guys."

But Robyn, not used to hiking, got confused about which way she was going. "Over here, I think." She led them over a small rise. "It was a big bear. And a little fisherman." But there was no stream on the other side. "No, wait. This way." She dashed off to the right, still describing the bear. "I'm sure I came this way. It was fumbling with the rod. And—and I thought I heard it talking. . . ." She trailed off when her friends started laughing again.

But about twenty minutes later—with no sign of any bear or fisherman—the Red Team lost its sense of humor. Nobody was the slightest bit afraid of bears now—not even Kelly. And even Ray and Louis had stopped joking about it.

Alex glanced at the sky. The sun had already sunk below the tops of the trees. "I can't believe how quickly it starts to get dark here in the woods."

"Scott," Annie said with a worried frown, "Alex is right. I think we should get back on the trail and head for camp."

"Right." Scott put his thumb and forefinger to his lips and whistled—loudly. The whole group stopped.

"Okay, everybody. It's time to quit fooling around and get back on the trail. We don't want to be out here when it gets dark."

"Especially with a bear wandering around," Robyn agreed.

Nicole shook her head. "Robyn, just drop it."

Scott started walking toward the sunset.

"Wait!" Kelly hollered. "Shouldn't we be

going the other way? I'm sure we came from that direction."

"Are you guys joking or what?" Louis demanded. "You're both wrong. We should be walking south of here. That way."

Alex looked around. She had no idea which way to go to get back to the trail.

But everyone else seemed to have a strong opinion.

Unfortunately, nobody agreed.

They tried one way.

They backtracked.

Still no bright red trail blazes.

The colors of the forest faded to gray.

Twilight.

In the growing darkness Alex stumbled over an exposed tree root. Her camera fell out of her jacket pocket. As she stuffed it back in, her eye was caught by the sticker across the bottom. It read "Courtesy of Paradise Valley Chemical Plant." The plant. The *plant!* Suddenly Alex had an image of a talking bear fumbling with a fishing rod. Maybe they weren't alone out here. Maybe Vince and Dave—

Alex noticed that everyone had stopped talking.

Everyone was walking closer and closer together.

One by one, flashlights flicked on.

And then darkness fell, as suddenly as if someone had dropped a curtain across the sun.

Alex ran to catch her sister and tell her what she was thinking about Vince. She could see her friends up ahead, their flashlights bobbing along in the darkness like a string of Christmas lights in the night.

We're walking around in circles *out here.*

And somewhere out here are Vince and Dave!

CHAPTER 8

The kids closed up into a little circle as Alex hurried up to them, flashlights in their faces, as if ready to tell ghost stories.

Louis spoke up. "Anybody got a pager? A cellular phone?"

The other kids just stared at him.

Louis shrugged. "Hey, I just wish I'd brought my dad's."

"Speaking of dads, ours is probably going crazy with worry," Annie said.

"We'll be okay," Nicole said. "Your parents know we can take care of ourselves."

"What do we do now?" Alex asked. "Scott?"

Scott looked around him. He paused a moment, thinking. "I think the best thing we can do now is make camp," he finally said. "People camp out in the woods like this all the time. We're in a pretty safe area. We've got food. Right, Norman?"

Norman swallowed. "Uh, I think we've got some stuff left."

"And if everybody brought standard emergency supplies, we should be fine."

"I don't agree," Kelly said. "No one will know we're okay. There's got to be a trail around here somewhere. This is a state park!"

"Maybe Kelly's right," Louis said. "Maybe we *should* keep going—we might stumble across a trail. Eventually."

"I understand how you feel," Scott said. "But it's not smart to go wandering around in the dark. It's tough to see in unfamiliar territory, even with flashlights. Somebody could get hurt. All my wilderness training suggests that the safest, smartest thing to do now is to make camp, sit tight, and wait for the sun to come up—or to be rescued."

"That's right," Annie said. "And I'm sure the grown-ups are out looking for us right now."

Alex tried to catch Annie's eye.

Scott nodded. "Annie's right. Now, who's got—"

"Does this mean you're not coming?" Kelly interrupted.

Scott blinked in surprise. "That's right," he said patiently.

Kelly looked stunned.

"Uh-oh," Nicole whispered to Alex. "Miss Used to Getting Her Own Way just got shot down."

"Fine, then!" Kelly exclaimed. "But I'm not going to sit around here all night." And with that, she headed off determinedly into the woods.

"Kelly, wait—stop!" Scott shouted.

But Kelly kept running.

Scott started after her. Then they heard Kelly stumble and crash.

And scream!

Scott bolted into the darkness.

Alex ran right behind him. It was difficult to see.

Suddenly Scott stopped dead in his tracks.

Alex crashed into his back.

"Alex, look out!"

Alex stopped and looked.

Scott shone his flashlight just past the toes of his hiking boots.

He'd stopped a few inches from a dropoff into a steep ravine!

CHAPTER 9

They both took a deep breath.

"Close call, huh?" Scott looked at Alex with relief.

"Yeah! Thanks—" She broke off when she heard Kelly clear her throat.

"Over here, Scott!" Kelly was sitting on the ground near a large rock. "I think I broke my ankle."

Alex and Scott hurried to her side.

Just then the other kids came up behind them.

"What happened?"

"Where's Kelly?"

"What's going on?"

"Listen, Kelly," Scott was saying. "Can you stand up?"

"Ouch!"

Ray and Louis consulted with Scott.

Alex and Nicole helped Kelly over to a fallen log so she could sit down.

Annie gently removed Kelly's brand-new hiking boot, now scuffed and skinned by the fall, and checked her ankle. "Yes, I think it's probably sprained. But luckily it's not broken." She pulled the first-aid kit out of her backpack and wrapped Kelly's ankle in an Ace bandage.

Meanwhile, Ray and Louis searched the nearby area and found a large, sturdy piece of wood with a rough Y shape at one end.

"What's that for?" Norman asked.

"Watch!" Ray said.

He wrapped the bare wood of the Y with a spare T-shirt from his pack. Then he secured it with another Ace bandage.

"Not bad for a homemade crutch, huh?" Ray said proudly.

"Cool!" Scott exclaimed. "How'd you think of that?"

Alex giggled. "Ray and I used to play wounded soldier when we were little."

Annie helped Kelly stand up, and Alex slipped the crutch under her arm. "How's that feel?"

Kelly wrinkled her nose. "Okay, I guess."

Alex shrugged and turned away. She figured Kelly must be pretty embarrassed.

Then Scott took charge. He led the group a short way to a fairly nice clearing. "Lucky for us it's a clear night with a nearly full moon."

Quickly they set up an emergency camp using supplies from their packs. A tarp for the ground, some rope, and everybody's rain ponchos made a couple of pretty decent shelters. Everyone helped gather kindling and firewood.

But Scott had trouble starting a fire.

"Let me try," Alex said.

"Okay," Scott said, stepping back.

Alex leaned in close, pretending to fiddle with matches and kindling. But, instead, she made a few quick, tiny zaps that quickly started a fire.

Annie, as usual, shot her a warning glance.

Oops! Alex thought. *And Annie doesn't even know about Vince and Dave yet!*

Ray smiled knowingly. "Way to go, Alex."

Soon everyone was settled around a nice, cheery fire.

Dinner was granola bars—the ones Norman hadn't already eaten—plus crackers and juice boxes. Nicole had also brought along a coffee can of traditional trail mix called GORP—Good Old Raisins and Peanuts. But her GORP also had M&M's. It made a great dessert!

Kelly's ankle was hurting her, so Annie advised her to lie down under the lean-to and go to sleep.

"Wake me up if we get rescued," Kelly said.

They all stared into the crackling fire for a while. Alex tried to think of a way to get Annie away from the group.

Finally Robyn, who'd been pretty quiet the last few hours, spoke up. "I, uh, guess I owe everybody an apology. For getting us all lost in the first place."

Nicole patted her buddy on the back. "That's okay, Robyn."

"No, really. I know you don't believe me, but I did see that bear—"

"Here we go again!" Louis joked.

Robyn shot him a look, then said, "Still, if I hadn't wandered off the trail in the first place, I never would have seen it, and none of this would have happened."

"Apology accepted," Scott said.

Robyn smiled, but she still looked embarrassed.

"Hey, Scott," Alex piped up. "When it said 'Challenge Yourself' on the Explorations sign-up poster, it wasn't kidding!"

Scott laughed. "Well, we certainly didn't plan on all this."

"But you know what?" Ray said. "This is pretty cool. I've never been camping like this before."

Annie came around, collecting everyone's trash to bag up.

Alex then whispered to her, "We gotta talk!"

"Okay," Annie said. "But wait till everyone's asleep."

"I've got an idea," Louis said suddenly. "How about we tell ghost stories?"

"Yeah!" Ray agreed, "Do you know the one about the couple whose car broke down in the woods—"

"You mean the one with the bloody hook on the door handle?" Louis asked. "That's my favorite! Especially the part when—"

"Guys!" Alex interrupted. She didn't like ghost stories to begin with. Her life was scary enough—what with showering in toxic chemicals and being chased by Vince and Dave. "Maybe some other time?"

"I agree," Robyn said. "Like, isn't this scary enough for you guys without making things up?"

Everyone agreed with that!

One by one the kids began to doze off. Some lay down under the shelter.

Norman fell asleep against a tree, with the last granola bar in his hand.

But Alex wasn't sleepy yet. Partly because she didn't want to have any more dreams out in the open!

"Your parents must be frantic," Scott said.

Alex nodded. "Do you think they're looking for us?"

"Maybe. Or they might wait till morning. Mr. Hendricks knows I'm pretty experienced."

Annie got up from her spot by the fire. "Hey, Ray—want to help me get some more firewood?"

Ray looked at the pile of wood. "Don't you think that's enough?"

Annie nodded her head toward Alex and Scott, as if to say, *Get my drift?*

"Oh, right," Ray said, grinning. "We should probably keep the fire going all night—in case they're out looking for us."

Waving over his shoulder at Alex, Ray followed Annie into the woods.

Alex almost laughed out loud. Was her big sister actually scheming to give her time alone with Scott? She couldn't believe it! *I think Bryce is definitely a good influence on her!*

"Are you having a good time?" Scott asked Alex.

"Good time?" Alex laughed. "Well, I'm not sure those are the exact words I'd use . . . but, yeah, I am. I had no idea when I signed up for this trip that it would be such an adventure!"

Scott laughed. "They're usually a little tamer than this." He picked up a stick and poked at the fire. "But you're really holding your own out here, Alex. I'm impressed. Do you camp and hike a lot?"

"Never," Alex admitted.

"Really? Maybe you should. You're pretty good at it." He shook his head. "Sometimes I think I'd rather sleep out under the stars than in my own room at home."

Just then Annie and Ray came crashing back into camp.

"Alex—" Annie smiled nervously. "Um, would you help us get more firewood?"

"Huh?"

"I'd be glad to help," Scott said, starting to get up.

But Ray shoved him back down. "No, no, no, *you* stay. We need you to stand watch. Alex wants to help. Don't you, Alex?"

He and Annie each grabbed one of Alex's arms and yanked her up.

"Annie—Ray! What in the world—?"

"We'll be right back," Annie told Scott with a big smile.

Alex reluctantly went along with them. "Annie, what has gotten into you? Are you crazy?"

"Quiet, Alex!" Annie hissed. "We've got something to show you. It's important!"

"Well, good, 'cause I need to—hey, slow down—!"

Annie and Ray dragged Alex along an overgrown path toward a slight hill.

At the top they ducked behind a rock.

"Why are we hiding?" Alex whispered.

Annie pointed. "Look!"

Halfway down the hill Alex spotted a tiny wooden cabin, its windows aglow.

Alex glanced at her sister. "So? What's that? A ranger's cabin or something?"

"Uh-uh," Ray said. "We thought it might be, too. So we went there, looking for help."

"But guess who we saw at the window—just in time," Annie said.

"Mr. Ranger?"

"Vince!"

"Oh, no! I was right!" Alex exclaimed. "I thought the fishing bear sounded too weird! I bet it's Vince and Dave!"

Annie nodded. "But what's he doing out here?"

"Remember who the sponsor is for the Science and Nature Club?" Ray asked.

"Danielle Atron and Paradise Valley Chemical!"

"Is he still in there?" Alex asked.

"No," Ray said. "He came out and headed that way." He pointed past the cabin.

They watched the cabin for a while, but it appeared to be empty, even though the lights had been left on.

"Come on," Alex whispered. "I want to find out what he's up to."

"Alex, wait—" Annie said.

But Alex had already sneaked up toward the cabin. Slowly she inched up toward the window to peek inside just as Annie and Ray joined her.

"It's empty," Alex confirmed. "I'm going inside to investigate."

"We'll stand guard," Ray said.

"Be careful!" Annie warned.

Alex sneaked up on the porch and slowly opened the door—just in case.

But there were no surprises hiding behind the door.

Shutting the door behind her, Alex glanced around.

It looks like the command center for the space shuttle! Alex thought. She took a closer look. *Make that a yard sale for the space shuttle. What is all this junk?*

Red lights blipped steadily on some kind of monitoring device. On another electronic screen, a glowing green hand swept around a dial like a one-armed clock. Gadgets and gizmos littered the tabletop.

Alex picked up a red file folder and looked inside. Paradise Valley Chemical stationery, with detailed typed notes about the Science and Nature Club outing. There was even a list of phone numbers and addresses for all the kids who signed up.

Including the names:

Mack, Alexandra
Mack, Annie
Mack, Barbara
Mack, George

Vince and Dave must be out here looking for the GC 161 kid.

Alex gulped. *Don't they ever give it a rest?* she

wondered. She'd thought she wouldn't have to worry about them on this trip. But they'd been out there, dressed as a fisherman and a bear, spying on all the kids the whole time!

Now what? Alex wondered.

Suddenly she saw Annie's and Ray's faces in the window. They were waving at her.

Alex frowned. *Uh-oh. Trouble.*

Stomp, stomp!

Heavy footsteps—right outside on the front porch.

Alex stared at the window. *Uh-oh!*

Annie and Ray waved at her like crazy, mouthing the words, *Get down! Hide!*

Alex frantically glanced around the room.

Small room.

No place to hide.

Quick! she told herself.

Alex closed her eyes, with her arms at her sides, even as she heard coughing and then a big sneeze outside.

The last thing she saw was Annie's face—looking as if she were about to faint!

Alex thought of water: *streams, showers, rainfall, and drizzle . . .*

She'd morphed dozens of times before, but never this fast—

Raindrops, swimming pools, lemon-lime seltzer . . .

And then a familiar tingle washed over her, kind of like when her foot went to sleep, but without any pain—more like a tingle of excitement.

And then she was falling, sinking into herself, melting like the Wicked Witch of the West, only not hot but cool like mountain spring water . . .

Plop!

Into a smooth, silvery puddle.

The folder Alex had been holding smacked to the floor—

The door to the cabin slammed open—

Just as Alex slithered across the floor into the corner, beneath the desk.

"Where *is* he!" Vince shouted, slamming the door closed.

He dragged out the chair and sat down at the table.

Alex swooshed up against the wall as Vince's heavy boots stretched toward her beneath the table.

"Dave—Dave, can you hear me? Come in, Dave."

He must be talking on a walkie-talkie.

"Dave! We don't have time to play games. Are you hiding? Are you lost?" Vince's fingers drummed on the tabletop above Alex. "Da-ave. Tell me where you are, and I can come get you."

Still no answer.

"I give up!" Vince wailed.

Go look for him! Alex silently begged. Five minutes was the most that she could remain in her morphed condition.

But Vince didn't leave. He turned in his seat. Alex heard him flicking switches, punching buttons.

Bleep bleep bleep!

Across the room some kind of monitor began to beep like crazy. Vince jumped up and ran to look. Now Alex could see him.

"He—he's here!" Vince exclaimed. "My GC 161 kid is here somewhere!" He ripped the park map from the wall and studied it. Then he glanced back at the screen. "And he's close by." Vince threw back his head and laughed. "I can't believe it! I'm actually going to get my hands on that kid tonight!''

Alex felt a strong sensation—something like a major burp—gush up right through her middle.

Bummer!

It was her warning that she was about to turn back into Alex Mack—the fourteen-year-old-girl variety—

Right in front of Vince's evil ice-blue eyes!

CHAPTER 10

Alex summoned all her strength and sluiced up the wall like some kind of alien jellyfish. Hoping that Vince would keep his back to her, she slid past several of the devices and then ran back down the wall to the floor.

Beep beep beep!

Blip-blip-blip-blip!

Riiiiing!

Alex had activated several alarms at once. But would it be enough to confuse him?

"Wait a minute. What's going on here?" Vince dashed from one to the other, staring at the screens, trying to make sense of the signals. "Oh, forget it—who cares? The kid's right outside somewhere. All I gotta do is run out and grab him!"

Giggling hysterically, Vince dashed outside and ran off.

Three seconds later Alex felt as if she were being swept *up* a waterfall against her will . . .

And then she was Alex once more, huddled beneath the table.

For a moment she couldn't move. *That was way too close.*

Then she wriggled out from under the table and stood up.

Now what?

Her next step was obvious. She had to put these gadgets out of business.

Alex raised her right hand. *Zap! Zap! Zap!*

A minute later Vince's gadgets lay ruined, like a roomful of busted toys the day after Christmas.

Alex dashed for the door.

Then she stopped. She tossed one more *zap!* over her shoulder at the overhead light.

The room was plunged into darkness.

And Alex ran out into the night.

Vince's command center was officially shut down.

Around back, Ray had his arm around a very nervous-looking Annie. "We saw everything!" Ray whispered. "Nice work, Alex."

"Alex!" Annie hissed. "Next time, pay more attention. What would I do if something happened to you?"

"Ah, yes," Ray quipped. "Another touching family moment for the Mack sisters!"

The girls laughed.

Then Annie's face turned serious again. "It's not safe to be out here," she said. "Not with vermin like Vince creeping around."

"But what can we do?" Alex said. "We're stuck here till morning."

"Or till somebody finds us," Ray pointed out. "Hey, Alex, remember that time after the dance last year? You know, when we went out to that field and you zapped the sky full of fireworks?"

"You did *what?*" Annie gasped.

"Oh, uh, that was nothing, Annie," Alex said quickly. "I'll tell you about it later."

"You could do that now," Ray suggested. "It

would be like sending up emergency flares. The rangers or your folks are bound to see them if they're looking for us."

"But what if Vince sees them, too?" Annie pointed out. "He and Dave are around here somewhere. With new *detectors.*"

Ray shrugged. "I still think we should risk it."

"Well, whatever we do, we need to get away from this cabin before Vince comes back," Alex told them.

They hurried back toward their emergency camp. In the distance they could see the campfire. Scott was pacing back and forth, stopping every now and then to peer off into the darkness.

"Do you think he's looking for *us?*" Alex whispered.

"Maybe. Look, Ray, you go with Alex. Find a good spot nearby—but where nobody will actually see what Alex is doing. I'll go distract Scott somehow. I think everybody else is asleep."

Annie hurried over to the campfire and sat down next to Scott.

"Hey!" Scott said. "I've been worried about you guys. Where's Alex?" He looked around.

"And ... Ray?" Then he looked at Annie's empty arms. "And where's the firewood?"

"Oh, uh—" Annie blushed. "Well, you see, I sort of got tired, and, of course, we didn't want you to worry, so I came back, and, um ..." Annie took a deep breath. "Ray and Alex will be back in a few minutes." She smiled innocently.

"What are they saying?" Alex said, peeking over Ray's shoulder at Annie and Scott.

"I can't hear a thing," Ray said. "But it looks like she's got him distracted. Come on, let's get the fireworks going!"

Alex and Ray slipped off to a small break in the trees.

Alex stood in the middle and stared at the sky. It was a bright, clear night. All the clouds had disappeared. She noticed a familiar pattern in the stars, but she couldn't remember the name of the constellation.

She raised both hands, fingers extended. With a flick of her wrists, lights shot from her fingertips into the sky like Roman candles.

"Can you arc them?" Ray asked. "So they look like shooting stars or a meteor shower?"

"I'll try. Maybe they'll all come here for a better look." Alex wiggled her fingers a bit. The flashes trailed off over their makeshift campsite.

"Wow!" Ray breathed, shaking his head in amazement

Alex grinned. It was one of her most magical powers. "I wonder if I'll always be able to do this? Maybe it will wear off one day. Or maybe Annie will think up a way to cure me!"

"Who knows? You'll still be the same Alex," he assured her. "But it's pretty cool getting to be your best friend while you can do stuff like this!"

Alex shot more flares into the sky, allowing several minutes in between. Off in the distance she could see Scott and Annie on their feet, pointing up at the sky in wonderment.

"How long do you think I should keep doing this?" Alex wondered.

Ray sat back against a tree. "We haven't got anything better to do. All night, as far as I'm concerned. Or until we get rescued."

Or, Alex thought, *till Vince uses it to track me down.*

CHAPTER 11

"I bizm a drodnikus," Ray mumbled.

Alex giggled. Ray had dozed off, curled up like a puppy against a tree, and was talking in his sleep.

Alex was still walking around the clearing, zapping the sky about every five minutes.

"Azshzit, too?"

She had no idea what he was talking about. It sounded like he was dreaming about an episode of *Star Trek* and was trying to talk to aliens!

Alex yawned. It was weird to be sort of by yourself out in the woods in the middle of the night. She was usually pretty scared of the dark. So she was surprised she felt so calm and safe. Besides, the moon was nearly full, and she was amazed at how well she could see.

Alex glanced at her watch. It was late. *I'm probably the only one awake in the whole park. Maybe in the whole state!*

She zapped another flare, and just this once she risked making a tiny little curlicue loop at the end.

She had a sudden urge to scrawl "Welcome to the Secret Life of Alex Mack" across the sky in ten-foot-tall cursive letters. To shower the darkness with her very own Fourth of July fireworks display and shout, "See what I can do?"

Maybe one day she'd be able to share her powers with the world. But not tonight.

Suddenly Alex heard an engine.

Some kind of vehicle was coming.

Was it a park ranger? Her dad?

Or Vince?

She ran over and shook Ray awake.

"Who? What?" Ray jumped to his feet.

"It's okay, Ray," Alex said. "It's me. But somebody's coming. Listen!"

Ray woke up completely when he heard the motor. "Come on!"

He dragged Alex toward their camp.

Annie had fallen asleep next to the fire.

But Scott was still awake, sitting on the ground, staring at the sky.

Uh-oh, Alex thought. *Did he see my scribbles in the sky? I'm glad I didn't write my name!*

But somehow she felt she wouldn't be too worried if he had. He seemed like the kind of person who would keep an important secret like that.

As she and Ray ran into the circle of firelight, Scott jumped to his feet. "Alex! Ray! Where've you been?" He pointed to the sky. "Did you see the flares?"

"Um, yeah," Alex said. "Pretty weird, huh? But listen, Scott. Somebody's coming! Annie, wake up!"

Annie sat up sleepily as the others listened.

"It's a Jeep!" Scott exclaimed. He glanced around, peering into the darkness. "Look! Head-lights!" He pointed up the rise a bit to where the vehicle had stopped, prevented from coming closer by the dense woods.

Annie jumped up and put her arm around Alex just as headlights blinded them all.

Somebody had found them—at last.

But who?

"Annie! Alex! Thank God you're all right!"

"Dad!" Alex shouted, and ran toward the car.

She and Annie were in their father's arms. "Everyone's been so worried," Mr. Mack said. "All your mother could say all night was 'We should have gone to the dude ranch. We should have gone to the dude ranch.'"

The girls laughed.

Mr. Hendricks and a park ranger climbed out of the Jeep, too. The ranger was carrying a first-aid bag. "Is anyone here hurt?"

Scott stepped forward and shook the ranger's hand. "We've got one sprained ankle down in the clearing. But otherwise, we're all safe and sound."

"What happened, Scott?" Mr. Hendricks asked.

"It's a long story, sir," Scott said. "But basically, we got lost. After it got dark, we decided it would be safer to stay put till help arrived or the sun came up."

"Smart move," the ranger said. "But I don't know if we'd have found you before morning if you hadn't sent up those flares."

"Uh, that wasn't us, sir," Scott admitted.

"It wasn't? Then who—"

"I think it was that meteor shower they predicted," Annie said. "Weather cleared up after all. Isn't that right, Alex?"

"Uh, yeah. Just like you predicted, Dad."

The ranger reached into his Jeep for the mike to his CB. "I'll radio the others and let them know you're all right."

"Well, I'm glad I saw part of it. But I'm happier that you're both okay," George Mack said.

When they all got back to camp safe and sound, everyone celebrated around the campfire with hot chocolate. Now that the danger was all over, they could laugh at the stories the kids told.

"I think you all deserve double extra credit," Mr. Hendricks joked.

"Uh, Mr. Hendricks, could we get that in writing?" Ray asked.

Alex's group clapped and cheered their agreement.

Then Robyn even told about seeing what she'd really thought was a bear.

The ranger grinned. "Well, miss, I assure you, we haven't had a report of any bears in this park for at least, oh, ten years or more."

Robyn shrugged good-naturedly. "Maybe he was lost?"

Everybody laughed.

Suddenly they heard something crashing around in the woods.

A dark shape lumbered toward them from the darkness.

Robyn covered her face and screamed, "It's the bear! I just know it!"

Mrs. Mack put her arm around the frightened girl. "Honey, of course it's not a bear—"

Then Barbara Mack's mouth fell open and her eyes popped wide—just like everybody else sitting around the fire.

Standing right in front of them, looking ferocious in the firelight, was a bear!

CHAPTER 12

Alex jumped to her feet, planning to throw up a force field and stop the bear in its tracks. But before she could do that, the bear did something amazing.

He yanked off his furry head.

"Uh, hi, kids. Does anybody know where the ranger station is?"

"Dave?" Mr. Mack said, coming slowly to his feet. "Is that you?"

"Oh, uh, hi, Mr. Mack." Dave grinned. "Yup, it's me."

"Well, what are you doing out here in the middle of the night dressed like that?"

Dave looked up a moment, as if he were trying to read something on his forehead. "Uh, I'm out here working on eco-friendly promos for the plant and our continuing commitment to nature and the park service." Dave grinned. "I play the bear."

"Do you have the feeling Vince made him memorize that line?" Alex whispered to Annie.

"Definitely," her sister agreed.

"Anyway," Dave went on, "I got lost."

The ranger stepped forward, putting his hat back on. "I'll be glad to give you a ride. It'll give me a chance to ask you a few questions. And you"—he turned to Kelly—"should come with me for a little first aid."

He led Dave to his car.

"Great!" Dave cried. He jumped into the Jeep.

Kelly climbed in after him. "See you tomorrow," she called to Scott as they drove off.

The ranger slid into the driver's seat, shaking his head.

As they drove off, Louis smiled. "That's the most cheerful bear I've ever seen."

"I guess he was the bear I saw," Robyn admitted. "But what about the fisherman?"

Alex, Ray, and Annie exchanged a secret glance. They had a pretty good idea who the fisherman was! Alex wondered where he was now.

It had been an exhausting night. Most of the campers headed off to their tents to try to catch some sleep before morning.

"I promise to let everyone sleep an extra fifteen minutes," Mr. Hendricks said.

Everyone glared at him.

Mr. Hendricks threw up his hands. "It's a joke! I was kidding! Sleep as late as you like. But don't forget what we have scheduled tomorrow ..."

"Tubing on the river!" Ray shouted. "All *right!*"

Alex walked with her sister and friends back to their tent.

"Has this been one fabulous trip or what?" Nicole said.

Robyn groaned. "Give me a break."

"Oh, come on, Robyn," Alex said. "Didn't you have any fun?"

"Ehh, five minutes maybe." Robyn grinned.

"Maybe next time you guys will believe me when I warn you how dangerous camping is!" She climbed into her sleeping bag fully dressed. "Wake me when it's time to go home," she mumbled into her pillow.

"Good night, Robyn!" Nicole said, shaking her head at her friend. Then she, too, curled up under the covers. "Will the last person to bed please turn out the lights. . . ."

Alex and Annie crawled into their sleeping bags.

Neither spoke.

"Annie," Alex whispered at last.

"What?"

"I'm glad you're my sister. Thanks for the help."

"No problem. That's what big sisters are for."

"Sure!" Alex grinned into the darkness. "By the way, Annie, why did you tell them it was the meteor shower?"

"Because, silly, if they thought somebody else was lost and signaling for help, we might have been out there all night. And I wanted to get back and go to sleep! Good night, Alex!"

"Good night, Annie!"

But Alex couldn't go to sleep. She was too wound up. All she could think about was how close she'd come to becoming one of Paradise Valley's lab rats tonight. Who knew what weird stuff might be happening to her—right now?

One day soon, Annie, Alex thought, *we're gonna have to tell Mom and Dad. . . .*

Alex sat up and noticed through the net window of the tent that the campfire was still going. Somebody was still up.

She crawled out and saw that it was her mom sitting by the fire, sipping hot chocolate, with a blanket wrapped around her shoulders. When she saw Alex, she held open the blanket with one arm. "Come here."

Alex scooted under the blanket with her mom. Mrs. Mack held up her cup. "Want some?"

"No, thanks."

"I'm glad you're okay," her mom said. "We were really worried. And yet, deep down, I knew you were okay."

"Really?"

"Yeah. You're a pretty reliable kid. You know that?"

Alex smiled and snuggled closer to her mom.

"Where's Dad?"

Barbara Mack pointed toward a small field several yards from the campsite. "Your dad wanted to see more of that meteor shower he planned to watch tonight. You know your dad and the stars." Mrs. Mack grinned. "Some of our first dates were a threesome: me, your dad, and his telescope."

But Alex saw another figure helping her dad set up his telescope. "Who's that with him?"

"Scott." Her mom put down her mug. "Come on. Let's go see what they're up to."

Alex's dad was peering into the telescope when they walked up. "Oh, wow. It's such a perfect night for looking at the stars."

Alex couldn't believe it. He didn't sound a bit sleepy.

When he looked up and saw Alex, he smiled. "Oh, hi, Alex. I was just telling Scott here—remember when you were little? We used to bundle you and Annie into the car and drive out into the country to look at the stars."

"That was back before we got so busy," Mrs. Mack added.

Alex had forgotten. But now, as she stood in

the field with the stars overhead, she remembered how her dad had once made science seem like magic and adventure. Before she even knew what the word *science* meant. Before science turned into something to fail at when you couldn't memorize what the teacher wanted.

"George," Mrs. Mack said, linking arms with her husband. "How about a moonlit stroll?"

"Now?" Mr. Mack said. "But, Barbara, I just set up the telescope."

"See that rock way over there? It's the perfect front-row seat for watching meteors."

"Uh, will you kids be okay till we get back?" Mr. Mack asked.

Alex watched her mom roll her eyes. "Yeah, Dad. We'll be fine."

Scott stepped back from the telescope. "Want to take a look?"

"Sure." Alex closed one eye and squinted into the eyepiece. The moon shone like a golden coin in the black sky. "Wow," she said softly. "It's so crisp and clear. And you can see the craters on the moon!"

"I thought you said you weren't so interested in science," Scott teased her.

"I'm not. I hate science. Besides, how could I compete with my dad or Annie? They're scientific geniuses."

"Do you like looking at the moon and the stars?"

"Yeah, I guess I do."

"And do you like camping out here in the woods?"

"Um-hmm."

"How about that little lizard we saw this afternoon? What did you think of him?"

"He was adorable!"

"Then you *don't* hate science. Because this"— Scott waved his arm at the sky . . .

"And this"—he swept his arm toward the trees and the fields . . .

"And Larry the Lizard are what science is all about." He folded his arms with a grin. "Besides, Alex, who said you have to compete with Annie and your dad? Can't you just like science for yourself?"

Alex laughed. "So what do you want to be when you grow up—a scientist or a guidance counselor!"

"Maybe both!"

"How'd you get so interested in science, anyway?"

"My grandfather," he answered.

"Is he a scientist?"

"Nah." Scott laughed softly. "He wasn't a scientist—for a career, at least. But he—well, it sounds kind of corny, but he loved nature. Really loved it. When I was little, he used to take me on these walks all the time. Man, he could tell you the name of every plant or tree or wildflower you ever saw. He knew all these folk legends about predicting weather. And he taught me about the constellations." Scott cleared his throat. "I really miss him."

Just then Alex saw her dad signaling them with his flashlight.

"What's he trying to tell us?" Alex said.

"Alex—look up! We almost missed it!"

The meteor shower—the *real* one—was spangling the night sky with shooting stars.

"It's fabulous!" Alex gasped.

Did her dad ever feel this way when he was slaving away at Paradise Valley Chemical for Danielle Atron? Did Annie, with her nose buried in scientific books and reports?

She looked at Scott. She could tell he did.

"Hey, I just remembered something my dad showed me about the moon when I was a little girl."

"Oh, yeah? What?"

"He didn't tell us about the man in the moon. He showed us how you can see the profile of a beautiful Victorian lady. Can you see it? Look. She's facing to the left. Her dark hair is pinned up in one of those old-fashioned hairdos, and her chin is lifted, like she's thrown her head back and is laughing."

Scott squinted at the moon. "Hey, I can see her! Cool!"

"Now, look just below her ear," Alex continued. "That's Tranquility Base, the spot where Neil Armstrong first set foot on the moon."

"Amazing," Scott said, shaking his head. "I'll never be able to look at the moon again without seeing that lady." He grinned at Alex. "Or thinking of you."

Alex stared wide-eyed at the sky and sighed.

So this was science, huh?

She thought she *hated* science.

And, well, she did hate Mr. Hendricks's tough, tricky tests that tied her up in knots.

Her dad's cold laboratory that smelled like chemicals and rotten eggs.

Annie's test tubes, charts, and graphs and all her great big words that Alex would need a brain transplant just to pronounce.

But maybe science was also the smell of trees sprouting new leaves on a warm spring night.

Astronauts landing on the cheek of a Victorian beauty.

The way her heart beat a little faster when watching shooting stars with Scott.

She'd always thought science was just books and beakers and formulas written in dusty chalk on a classroom blackboard.

But maybe it was also about the world Alex could touch and see and smell. Maybe it was about feelings, too.

Maybe there was some connection between what made the planets spin and what made her heart twirl.

But Alex didn't think she could count on Mr. Hendricks to teach her about that.

She glanced at Scott.

I think I'm going to have to figure this one out all by myself.

About the Author

Cathy East Dubowski thinks it would be fun to relive eighth grade—especially if she could morph and zap like Alex Mack and have a best friend like Ray. Writing *Take a Hike!* was the next best thing.

Cathy has written more than thirty-five books for kids, including several in the Full House series published by Minstrel Books. One of her books for younger readers, *Cave Boy*, was named an International Reading Association Children's Choice.

Cathy lives in North Carolina, where she enjoys hiking in the Appalachian Mountains and stargazing while camping on the Outer Banks. Her favorite hiking buddies are her husband, Mark Dubowski, a cartoonist and children's book illustrator, her daughters, Lauren and Megan, and their big red golden retriever, Mac-Dougal. Her favorite constellation is Orion.

A MINSTREL® BOOK